W9-BUT-381

THE FERRYMAN

JEZ BUTTERWORTH

THEATRE COMMUNICATIONS GROUP
NEW YORK
2017

The Ferryman is published by Theatre Communications Group, Inc., 520 Eighth Avenue, 24th Floor, New York, NY 10018-4156

This volume is published in arrangement with Nick Hern Books Limited, The Glasshouse, 49a Goldhawk Road, London, W12 8QP

This publication is made possible in part by the New York State Council on the Arts with the support of Governor Andrew Cuomo and the New York State Legislature.

TCG books are exclusively distributed to the book trade by Consortium Book Sales and Distribution.

A catalogue record for this book is available from the Library of Congress.

ISBN 978-1-55936-566-6 (paperback)

Cover image by Dewynters

First TCG Edition, September 2017

THE FERRYMAN

The Ferryman was developed by Sonia Friedman Productions, and premiered at the Jerwood Theatre Downstairs at the Royal Court Theatre, London, on 24 April 2017. It was subsequently transferred to the Gielgud Theatre, London, on 20 June 2017 by Sonia Friedman Productions, Neal Street Productions & Royal Court Theatre Productions with Rupert Gavin, Gavin Kalin Productions, Ron Kastner and Tulchin Bartner Productions.

The West End cast (in order of appearance) was as follows:

LAWRENCE MALONE	Turlough Convery
FRANK MAGENNIS	Eugene O'Hare
FATHER HORRIGAN	Gerard Horan
MULDOON	Stuart Graham
QUINN CARNEY	Paddy Considine
CAITLIN CARNEY	Laura Donnelly
MERCY CARNEY	Elise Alexandre, Meibh Campbell, Scarlett Jolly
NUNU (NUALA) CARNEY	Angel O'Callaghan, Isla Griffiths, Clara Murphy
AUNT MAGGIE FARAWAY	Bríd Brennan
SHENA CARNEY	Carla Langley
UNCLE PATRICK CARNEY	Des McAleer
JAMES JOSEPH (JJ) CARNEY	Niall Wright
HONOR CARNEY	Sophia Ally, Grace Doherty, Amy Jayne
OISIN CARNEY	Rob Malone
AUNT PATRICIA CARNEY	Dearbhla Molloy
TOM KETTLE	John Hodgkinson
MICHAEL CARNEY	Fra Fee
MARY CARNEY	Genevieve O'Reilly
SHANE CORCORAN	Tom Glynn-Carney
DIARMAID CORCORAN	Conor MacNeill
DECLAN CORCORAN	Oliver Finnegan, Michael McCarthy, Jack Nuttall

Director	Sam Mendes
Designer	Rob Howell
Lighting Designer	Peter Mumford
Composer & Sound Designer	Nick Powell
Casting Director	Amy Ball CDG

For Fred Specktor

When I come to die,
I ask of you one favour,
That with the braids of your black hair
They tie my hands.

Traditional flamenco siguiriya

CHARACTERS

QUINN CARNEY, *forties*
MARY CARNEY, *late thirties, his wife*
CAITLIN CARNEY, *early thirties, Quinn's sister-in-law*
AUNT PATRICIA CARNEY, *eighties, Quinn's aunt*
UNCLE PATRICK CARNEY, *seventies, Quinn's uncle*
AUNT MAGGIE FARAWAY, *eighties, Quinn's aunt*
MULDOON, *forties, from Derry*
FRANK MAGENNIS, *twenties, from Derry*
LAWRENCE MALONE, *twenties, from Derry*
TOM KETTLE, *forties, an English factotum*
FATHER HORRIGAN, *fifties, a priest*
JAMES JOSEPH (JJ) CARNEY, *sixteen, Quinn and Mary's eldest son*
MICHAEL CARNEY, *fifteen*
SHENA CARNEY, *fourteen*
NUNU (NUALA) CARNEY, *eleven*
MERCY CARNEY, *nine*
HONOR CARNEY, *seven*
OISIN CARNEY, *fourteen, Caitlin's only son*
SHANE CORCORAN, *seventeen*
DIARMAID CORCORAN, *sixteen*
DECLAN CORCORAN, *thirteen*

Also, Bobby Carney, nine months, Quinn and Mary's newborn child

SETTING

The play is set in rural County Armagh, Northern Ireland, late August 1981.

The Prologue takes place in Derry, the previous day.

PROLOGUE

An alley in Bogside, Derry.

Back of a building. The wall is painted with Republican graffiti.

At one end stands LAWRENCE MALONE, *smoking, watching the street beyond.*

In the centre, FRANK MAGENNIS, *reading a paper.*

Near one side, a door in the wall, to the building beyond.

MALONE.
'Cease, cease with all your drumming,
All your whoring, all your mumming,
By my smell I can tell
A Priest this way is coming.'

Enter FATHER HORRIGAN.

He passes MALONE, *and approaches* MAGENNIS.

MAGENNIS. Morning, Father. Please…

MAGENNIS *indicates the priest to come closer.*
HORRIGAN *does.*

How was your journey?

HORRIGAN. I'm sorry I'm late.

MAGENNIS. Did you drive up?

HORRIGAN. I caught the bus.

MAGENNIS. Which bus is that now?

HORRIGAN. The 5D. Then the 8A from Sixmilecross into Waterside.

MAGENNIS. How long a journey is that?

HORRIGAN. All told? Roughly two hours.

MAGENNIS. Well, it must be beautiful down where you are this time of year. Harvest time and all.

HORRIGAN. Forgive me, why am I here?

Beat.

MAGENNIS. When I was a kid we used to go out to my grandfather's place down in Fermanagh there, and help with the harvest. It was good craic. Got us out the smoke. Out in the fresh air. Harvest time's a fine time of the year, so it is.

Pause.

Well, I'll get straight to it. (*Beat.*) Three days ago, there's two turf-cutters cutting turf in County Louth, just across the border there, when they come across a body in the bog. (*Beat.*) Now they've read the stories in the press about prehistoric finds, your Stoneyisland Man, your Tollund Man there, two thousand years old, and how the people that find them become famous. They're hatching all these dreams, TV interviews, prize from the National Museum and whatnot, when one of 'em spots that your man's wearing a pair of Gola trainers. A Timex wristwatch. Brown corduroys. (*Beat.*) So they rummage through his pockets and they find his car keys. His last pay packet from December 1971. Some Polos. A betting slip signed on the back by Georgie Best. A picture of his wee'un. (*Beat.*) So your two Herberts there call the Garda, and they run a quick check of your man's dental records, and they come up with a name.

He takes a photograph out of his pocket. Leans forward and hands it to HORRIGAN.

Do you know that man, Father? The fella standing on the left.

HORRIGAN *puts on his glasses. He studies the picture.*

HORRIGAN. His name is Seamus Carney.

MAGENNIS. And who's that fella standing on the right there?

Pause.

HORRIGAN. That's me.

MAGENNIS. That's grand. (*Takes the picture back*.) Now, Father, what can you tell me about your man there? What can you remember about Seamus Carney?

Pause.

HORRIGAN. Seamus disappeared ten years ago. 1972. New Year's Day 1972. He was twenty years old.

MAGENNIS. Disappeared…

HORRIGAN. He left for work. Got in his car, drove off. And disappeared. The story was he'd gone to Liverpool. That was the story.

MAGENNIS. Anything else?

HORRIGAN. Seamus was in the IRA. The rumour at the time was that he was an informer.

MAGENNIS. He left a young wife back there.

HORRIGAN. And a son. Three years old.

MAGENNIS. I take it you know them well. The family.

HORRIGAN. I've known the Carneys all my life. I knew their father and mother. I'm their priest.

MAGENNIS *hands* HORRIGAN *another photograph*.

MAGENNIS. This is a police photograph of Seamus Carney as they found him on Tuesday.

HORRIGAN *puts his glasses back on and looks at the photograph*.

The bog water turns a body black, but it preserves it. You see, Father, there's no oxygen down there. The peat is acidic. It pickles you. The years roll by and nothing changes. Did you know, Father, that when they found the Tollund Man, that *his* hands and feet were bound too. I wonder what went on there. What went down all the way back then. Can you see he's holding the rosary beads there?

HORRIGAN. I can. I can also see his wedding ring, which his wife is still working to pay off today.

MAGENNIS. We need your help.

Beat.

HORRIGAN. Okay, listen –

MAGENNIS. I appreciate this is all somewhat sudden, and it's doubtless something you'll wish to reflect upon. But right now, before we do anything else, I just need to know, broadly, if you're of a mind to help us. (*Beat.*) Are you willing to do that, Father?

Pause.

HORRIGAN. I... Look –

MAGENNIS. It's a Yes or a No.

HORRIGAN. Listen... Wait a minute.

MAGENNIS. No. Not 'Listen'. Not 'Wait a fucking minute'. 'Yes' or 'no'.

HORRIGAN. For pity's sake. Do you not think you've caused the Carney family enough misery?

Pause. MAGENNIS *gets out another photograph.*

MAGENNIS. Who's that?

HORRIGAN. That's my sister.

MAGENNIS. And where is she there?

HORRIGAN. She's coming out of the Spar in Killclogher.

Pause.

MAGENNIS. Can you help us, Father?

Pause.

HORRIGAN *nods.*

MAGENNIS *walks to the door, knocks three times, then takes up a position at the other end of the alley and keeps a look-out.*

From the door, a man enters. This is MULDOON. *He comes and stands in front of the priest. Silence.*

MULDOON. Do you know who I am?

HORRIGAN. No.

Beat.

MULDOON. I'm going to ask you some questions, now, and I just want you to answer how you feel is best.

HORRIGAN. Okay.

MULDOON. Good. Do you know who I am?

Pause.

HORRIGAN. Yes.

Pause.

MULDOON. Seamus had a brother. An older brother.

HORRIGAN. Yes.

MULDOON. What's his name now?

HORRIGAN. His name is Quinn Carney.

MULDOON. What can you tell me about him?

HORRIGAN. Quinn Carney is a farmer. He farms fifty acres in the parish. He has a wife. A family, he's a good man…

MULDOON. Was he always a farmer?

HORRIGAN. With respect, sir, what game are we playing here? Sure, everyone knows who Quinn Carney is. Most of all you.

Beat.

MULDOON. You're his priest.

HORRIGAN. Yes.

MULDOON. He confesses to you. You hear his confession…

HORRIGAN. Yes.

MULDOON. Why don't you tell me everything you know about Quinn Carney?

Blackout. Music.

'Street Fighting Man' by The Rolling Stones, loud.

ACT ONE

The Carney home. 5.30 a.m. End of August 1981.

A farmhouse kitchen, in rural Northern Ireland, harvest time.

Flagstone floor. Wooden beams. Washing hanging high in rows. At the back, a large coal-fired range.

A sink and crockery board. A steep wooden staircase leads upstairs. On the walls are pinned countless children's drawings, photographs, swimming awards. A John Deere 1981 calendar. A rota for feeding the animals, on which are stuck photographs of children. An old, torn Rolling Stones poster from when the Stones played Belfast in 1965 (also covered in children's drawings, etc.). On another wall, almost completely obscured by pictures of children from communions, sports days, swimming galas, dancing competitions, is an old, very weathered Irish flag.

A door stage-right to the larder. A boot room at the back, beyond through which entrances are made from outside – so people are seen putting on coats there, sometimes boots, before entering and leaving to the yard outside.

Above the central fireplace at the back is an old farmhouse clock, next to which is a large dusty framed picture of Big Jack Carney. Along the shelf, under him (backed by a long knitted Celtic FC scarf), is an array of old soccer programmes, egg timers, an old squeeze box, an old hand-held fire extinguisher, an old biscuit tin, a foot-high dusty plastic model of George Harrison with his French horn from Yellow Submarine *(painted in psychedelic colours). Dozens of candles. Some birthday cards. A framed photograph of Brigitte Bardot in* Helen of Troy, *another of George Best.*

The shutters are closed. The curtains drawn. The room is full of smoke.

A tape playing on a big ghetto blaster. The Rolling Stones, quietly.

On the table, candles burn. A full ashtray. A bottle of Bushmills, two inches left.

Either side of the table, sit CAITLIN CARNEY *and* QUINN CARNEY, *both smoking, both playing Connect Four.*

QUINN. You're on a ship with The Rolling Stones, The Beatles and Led Zeppelin. It hits an iceberg. There's only room in the lifeboat for you plus one of those legendary combos. Three seconds. Go.

CAITLIN. Led Zeppelin.

QUINN. You have three seconds.

CAITLIN. I don't need three seconds.

QUINN. You'd save Led Zeppelin.

CAITLIN. I just did.

QUINN. The Stones. The *Beatles*. They're all going to drown. All those geniuses. And Bill Wyman. All gone. Because you saved Led Zeppelin.

He lights a cigarette off a candle, puts it down too near a table lamp, which catches fire.

CAITLIN. Stop me before I kill again.

QUINN. Well, Cait Carney. You've made a terrible mistake. An unrightable wrong.

CAITLIN. The lamp's on fire.

QUINN. Don't change the subject.

CAITLIN. I'm just pointing it out.

He goes to the drawers and roots around.

QUINN. Okay, let's just. May I? Please. Just quickly. (*On his fingers.*) *Sticky Fingers. Beggars Banquet. Let It Bleed...* The Stones could...

He finds what he's looking for. A small fire extinguisher.

Fuckin' John, Paul, George and Ringo could be sat there with you in the boat doing the whole of *Sergeant Pepper*, *just for you*, while you row 'em to safety. But *no*. Because you saved Led Zeppelin. You're sat there, in the lifeboat, listening to four wee pricks singing about Hobbits...

With one blast, he puts the fire out.

CAITLIN. You never said anything about music. You said who would I rather be stuck in a lifeboat with. If it's between Jimmy and Robert and all those other spotty wee fucks? If I can pick 'n' mix, Jimmy Page, Robert Plant, George Harrison, and Keith Richards. But he's going to have to have a fuckin' good wash first.

She drops in her counter.

One. Two. Three. Four.

She writes it down.

QUINN. Wait. Wait. What have you done? It was my go.

CAITLIN. That's seventeen plays one.

She releases the counters.

QUINN. You're a fuckin' cheat, Cait Carney.

CAITLIN. I don't have to cheat to beat you. Sure, I could beat you with a blindfold on.

QUINN. A pound.

CAITLIN. Done.

He gets up, fetches a tea towel. And blindfolds her.

QUINN. Here we go. Now we'll see. Now we'll find out who's the real champion. Who's got what it takes to put four coloured circles in a row. Before the other fella. Now then. Ready? I'll go first.

CAITLIN. It's my turn to go first.

QUINN. This is a new competition. The last one was abandoned. (*Fast, off her look.*) Shall I flip a coin? Heads or tails...?

CAITLIN. Tails.

He tosses an imaginary coin.

QUINN. Bad luck. It's heads. Best of three?

CAITLIN. Fuck it. I'll still win.

QUINN. Well, let's even it up. Let's make it an even playing field now. I don't want you griping after, saying it was unfair and all…

He gets another tea towel. Blindfolds himself.

Ready. Go.

They take turns. Until –

CAITLIN. Stop. I've won.

QUINN. How the fuck do you know that?

CAITLIN. Trust me. You've lost. (*Preparing to remove the blindfold.*) Ready? One, two –

QUINN. Wait! I don't want to take this off because I know I've fucking lost.

CAITLIN. Of course you've lost.

QUINN. Let's just stay like this. Let me just dream for a moment… Imagine what it feels like to have won. I just want to stay like this…

He lifts his glass.

CAITLIN. Cheers.

QUINN. Cheers.

They try to clink glasses. The music plays.

Caitlin Carney. Would you like to dance?

CAITLIN. Why thank you, Quinn Carney. That would be wonderful.

They stand. QUINN *goes over and turns the music up. And with their blindfolds on, they dance around the kitchen.*

QUINN *Jaggers along as the music builds.*

QUINN. Where are you?

CAITLIN. Over here.

He finds her.

QUINN. There you are.

They dance to the music. Together. Close.

In the dance, they separate.

QUINN *takes his blindfold off and looks at* CAITLIN, *dancing.*

He seems transfixed.

Enter MERCY CARNEY *from down the stairs.* QUINN *doesn't see her. He's only looking at* CAITLIN.

The song ends.

MERCY. What are you two doing?

QUINN *turns.* CAITLIN *removes her blindfold.*

QUINN. I could ask you the very same, young lady. What are you doing up? You should be in bed.

MERCY. It's morning.

QUINN. Don't be ridiculous.

MERCY. It's light out.

CAITLIN. She may have a point there.

QUINN. Right then. It's time to get up.

MERCY. I want to blow the horn.

QUINN. Oh, you do, do you?

MERCY. I want to blow the horn.

QUINN. Do you have the lungs? It's an important job.

MERCY. I'm ready.

QUINN. What do you think, Cait? You think she's ready?

CAITLIN. She says she's ready…

MERCY. I'm ready!

QUINN. Well, come on then. But you gotta do it right now. Are you ready? One two. Three.

She blows the horn. Loud. Fruity.

MERCY. It's morning!

QUINN. See, that's not bad. That's good enough to wake the dead, so it is.

MERCY (*bellows*). Everybody up!

CAITLIN *opens the curtains and shutters.* QUINN *fans the smoke out the door. Calls up the stairs.*

QUINN. MICHAEL CARNEY! GET YOUR ARSE OUT OF THAT SCRATCHER. THERE'S A GOOSE TO KILL!

QUINN *exits to the toilet. As –*

Enter NUNU (NUALA) CARNEY, *from upstairs, in her* Muppet Show *pyjamas.* MERCY *exits to the main part of the house.*

CAITLIN. Morning, Nunu…

NUNU. Honor Carney has eaten an entire bottle of vitamin-C tablets. And Oisin Carney said the F-word.

CAITLIN. Is that so?

NUNU. Then Michael Carney said the C-word. Then Oisin said the C-word back.

Re-enter MERCY *wheeling out an old lady in a 1920s wheelchair, a blanket on her knee.*

During the following, MERCY *positions the wheelchair in the room, where the old lady sits staring vaguely, benignly, out, as if trying to remember something just beyond her reach. This is* AUNT MAGGIE FARAWAY.

MERCY. What's the C-word?

CAITLIN. Never you mind.

NUNU. Morning, Aunt Maggie.

CAITLIN. Morning, Aunt Maggie. Did you sleep well now, Aunt Maggie?

She kisses her as she passes.

NUNU *and* MERCY *both kiss her, then go and put on aprons and begin making breakfast.*

Enter SHENA CARNEY *from upstairs, carrying her baby brother, singing the second verse of 'Ashes to Ashes' by David Bowie.*

That smock goes on the other way round. Buttons up the back.

SHENA. But they're such nice buttons. He'll be wanting to show 'em off for the photo.

CAITLIN. He doesn't want to spend eternity up on the wall there sat on a tractor dressed skew-whiff now.

SHENA. Look. He's got a fresh freckle.

CAITLIN. Where? (*Stops and looks.*) That's dirt. (*Licks her finger and wipes it off.*)

NUNU. Where's Dad?

CAITLIN. Getting washed.

NUNU. Has he killed the goose?

CAITLIN. Michael's killing the goose.

NUNU. Can we watch him kill it?

CAITLIN. If you're good.

Enter UNCLE PATRICK CARNEY, *from upstairs, in his old moth-eaten dressing gown.*

UNCLE PAT. In the beginning, all the gods were hunting gods. Then one day the Greeks discovered that the land was magical.

CAITLIN. Morning, Pat.

ALL. Morning, Uncle Pat.

UNCLE PAT. Good morning, Caitlin. Good morning to all.

MERCY. I want to crack the eggs.

CAITLIN. Well, get your wee apron on there.

CAITLIN *fills a bucket with soapy water.* UNCLE PAT *fixes himself a cup of tea.*

UNCLE PAT. Plant a seed and the seed would grow. And so the old gods died, and the new gods, the gods of the soil prevailed...

Enter JAMES JOSEPH (JJ) CARNEY, *from down the stairs, doing up his trousers.*

JJ. Morning, Aunt Cait. Morning, Aunt Maggie. Morning, Pat.

ALL. Morning, JJ.

UNCLE PAT. Hestia, the goddess of bread, Cyametes, she of the bean, Dionysis, him of the grape, and the mighty Demeter. Queen of all the Harvest...

JJ steals a piece of fried bread, a fried egg, folds it all up and takes a bite, and heads out to the boot room, where he pulls on his welly boots, puts on his coat and heads out.

CAITLIN (*to* SHENA). See if you can't get him off for thirty minutes. When he wakes up, fetch his scarf. And his bonnet. He's going blackberry-picking after.

UNCLE PAT. All Hail Demeter. Goddess of the Corn. Mother of the Harvest. You who made the first loaf, the bread our Saviour broke, and this here wee drop of Bushmills. *Sláinte!*

SHENA carries the baby upstairs, singing 'Ashes to Ashes' to him.

NUNU. Will you do me a French plait, Aunt Cait?

CAITLIN. It's on the list. (*To* UNCLE PAT.) Shift back here. Into the light.

UNCLE PAT shifts his chair a couple of feet, into the light. CAITLIN takes out a straight razor.

UNCLE PAT. I'd like to state for the record I had two ears and a nose going in.

CAITLIN (*to* UNCLE PAT). Keep still.

She begins soaping his face.

Enter HONOR CARNEY, *dressed as Cleopatra. From the top of the stairs, she calls:*

HONOR. Aunt Cait! Michael Carney just showed me his bumhole.

CAITLIN. And a 'Good Morning' to you too, Honor Carney.

HONOR. Not the bum mind. The *actual* hole.

CAITLIN. Keep still. Like trying to paint a pig, so it is.

OISIN CARNEY *has quietly entered from outside, and sits at the foot of the stairs, making a kite. Across the room,* MERCY *points to it.*

MERCY. What's that?

OISIN. The spine. This is the cross spar. That's the spine. It's like a skeleton. So when the wind takes it, it's ready. It all holds together.

MERCY. Will you teach us to fly him, Oisin?

HONOR. Can I go first?

MERCY. I want to go first!

HONOR. I'll go first and you go second.

MERCY. Can I go first, Oisin? Please?

OISIN. There might not be enough wind.

CAITLIN. There's wind all right. That northerly'll blow the whole day away.

UNCLE PAT. Now don't be putting too much Cow Gum on that fella, Oisin. Too much Cow Gum and she won't get off the ground.

OISIN. I know what I'm doing.

QUINN *re-enters from the toilet. Throughout the following – he washes his face in the sink, then fishes in a child's schoolbag, hanging on the wall. Among schoolbooks he finds a swimming towel (wrapped in it are a pair of goggles and a wet swimsuit), frees it, unfurls it and dries his face, etc.*

QUINN. Where's Michael?

CAITLIN. Flat on his cracker in bed.

QUINN. MICHAEL CARNEY. RISE AND SHINE!

MERCY. Daddy. Oisin's going to teach us to fly a kite.

HONOR. I'm going first and Mercy's goin' second.

MERCY. I'm going first!

QUINN (*to* NUNU, *ignoring the little ones*). Here, lass. Wet that. (*Hands her his mug. Washes his face in the sink.*)

HONOR. Will you come, Daddy? Please say you will.

MERCY. Please, Dad!

QUINN (*to* CAITLIN). What time are the Corcorans getting here?

CAITLIN. Any minute now. They're catching the first bus from Waterside.

He takes his mug back from NUNU.

QUINN. Give 'em a brew send 'em straight up Dunn's Ground. I'll meet 'em there with the combine. Where's Jim Joe?

CAITLIN. He blew through a minute back.

QUINN. Well, if you see him, tell him to stick a chainsaw on the trailer. Morning, Pat.

UNCLE PAT. I'm not allowed to move.

CAITLIN. Nunu, light the stove in the parlour, please.

NUNU. Yes, Aunt Cait.

Exit NUNU *into the parlour.*

MERCY. Will you come with us, Daddy? Up to the ridge?

Though his youngest daughters are pulling at his trousers, QUINN *acts like they're not even there.*

QUINN (*to* CAITLIN). Tell Tom to fill the tractor. The main tank's low so tell him to syphon what he can out the old drums by the silo. Did you ring Dermot's Diesel?

CAITLIN. Aye.

QUINN. And?

CAITLIN. Dermot's coming by at eight, but his mam says Dermot's been on the tear, so don't hold your breath.

MERCY. Daddy, please!

HONOR. Please, Daddy!

QUINN. Well, *if* he shows up tell him we're not paying the new price per gallon. There's enough banditry round here without… (*Suddenly stops.*) Wait. Stop. (*Looks down.*) Who's this? Who are you? Where did all these dwarves spring from?

MERCY. Dad –

HONOR. Dad, stop acting the nag.

QUINN. Hold your horses. I need names.

MERCY. Da-ad! (*Exasperated.*) I'm Mercy, she's Honor.

HONOR. No I'm not. I'm Cleopatra.

QUINN (*to* CAITLIN). Not the same Cleopatra who's the Queen of All Egypt?

CAITLIN. The very same.

QUINN. Well, that's a small world now. Because I'm that Julius Caesar fella, so I am.

MERCY (*trying to drag him to the kite*). Da-ad!

CAITLIN. Cleopatra's eaten a whole bottle of vitamin-C tablets…

QUINN. Is that so, Cleo? And how's that sitting with you?

HONOR. I'm not gonna lie, Julius. It's a wee bit fizzy in there.

QUINN. I bet it is.

MERCY. Dad, look!

QUINN. Wait. Hold on. (*Goes over to* OISIN.) What's goin' on here? What witchcraft is this?

MERCY. It's a kite, Dad!

QUINN. A what?

MERCY *and* HONOR. A *kite*!!

QUINN. I see. And what does a 'kite' do?

MERCY. Sure, you know what a kite does! It flies up to the sky!

QUINN. Impossible.

MERCY. It's not impossible. Oisin's made loads.

QUINN. Is this true, Oisin?

OISIN (*diffidently*). It's not mine. It's for the wee'uns…

QUINN. That's a cracking kite, so it is. (*Turns it over.*) All except for that. All except for the picture you got there.

OISIN. What picture?

QUINN. Can you see who that is there, Mercy?

MERCY. Shit the bed. That's Ian Paisley.

CAITLIN. Mercy Carney, mind your language.

OISIN. Where? Show me.

He does. Sure enough, Ian Paisley, looking furious.

QUINN. That's His Majesty, so it is. At full sail too.

OISIN (*defensive*). I never stuck that on there. Honor did.

HONOR. It's Cleopatra.

OISIN. Just give it back, would ya. Anyway, it's not finished.

QUINN. Get plenty of lacquer on him.

UNCLE PAT. Not too much Cow Gum.

QUINN. And get it nice and dry. There's a wind up today. With any luck, she'll fly. (*Shouts upstairs.*) MICHAEL CARNEY. THIS IS YOUR THIRD AND FINAL WARNING. GET YOUR LAZY ARSE OUT THAT SACK! YOU DON'T KEEP A LADY WAITING!

He heads out. CAITLIN *hands him a flask.*

Exit QUINN, *to the boot room, and out the door to the yard. During the following speech,* AUNT PATRICIA CARNEY *enters from downstairs. Over the following, she sets up a transistor with an earpiece, through which she listens.*

UNCLE PAT. Cow Gum! Now there's a scent to stir the soul. September, nineteen hundred and eleven... I was seven years old. Pat, Maggie, Arthur, Frank and me, all sharing a pallias in the stable, with fourteen cousins. It was one of those magical, crisp mornings, when the sun rises and softens all the sharp edges of the world. The whole house was heaving. Men, women, old ones, wee'uns. I was sat right there, on the slate, fettling my very own harvest kite. We had no newspaper, so it was a greaseproof contraption. Greaseproof paper, balsa wood, spit, prayer and God's own magic ingredient. Cow Gum!

AUNT PAT. Is anybody writing this down?

Beat.

UNCLE PAT. In those times, Oisin, there were no combines. Tractors. Just sweat and dust and horse and plough. Big Jack, the Burkes, the O'Connors, the McCools. All the men, all together. Bringing the harvest in.

NUNU *comes in from the parlour.*

AUNT PAT. Seriously, if nobody makes a note of this, it'll be lost for ever to the sands of time. Then where will we be? What a deep loss to humanity that would represent.

UNCLE PAT. I remember my very first Harvest Feast. This old kitchen was stiff to the rafters. Songs. Dancing. It was the very first time I ever tasted goose.

AUNT PAT. How many times have you heard this guff, Oisin? 'Uncle Pat's First Harvest'. You know what irks me most about this 'story'? *It isn't one.* There's absolutely no point to it. *Nothing happens.* No one gets drunk. No one feels up no one they shouldn't. No one falls into the grain silo and drowns. There's not even a good punch-up. There's a *kite*. And a *goose*. That's it. There's absolutely no point to it, except to say, 'Haven't I been around here a bleedin' long time, getting under the feet? Sixty straight harvests and I'm still clogging up the way.'

Beat.

UNCLE PAT. Big Jack's father there, at the head of that table. Brother Michael. Brother Frank. And your Great-Aunt Pat there, she was there too. My, she was a lovely little thing. Blonde ringlets. Violet eyes to trap the sunlight so, with a wee smile to make grown men gasp. Who would have thought that sweet little vision would grow into the twisted bitter gargoyle we see before us today. Bitter. Vicious. Reeking of piss from the neck down.

AUNT PAT. Think you're funny, Pat? You're about as funny as a feckin' orphanage on fire.

CAITLIN. You two. Mind your language. There's four sets of innocent ears right there.

OISIN. My ears aren't innocent. Sure, I've heard ten times worse at school.

CAITLIN. Well, you can learn it at school. You don't need any help from your elders and betters now.

AUNT PAT. SHUT UP. SHUT UP, EVERYONE. It's starting.

She listens.

CAITLIN. What's that about?

UNCLE PAT. Thatcher. On the World Service. She's due to make a statement this morning.

CAITLIN. Jesus. She'll get that ulcer back, so she will.

UNCLE PAT. She's been up half the night lying in wait for her. Honing her Battle Plan. I swear to God, sometimes I think the only thing keeping her alive is her hatred for that woman. You watch. Soon as Mrs T starts up, Pat'll be out of that chair screaming till she's blue in the bake, and *hopefully*, she'll have a massive coronary and drop stone dead on the flagstones there. Let's face it, it's how she'd want to go. Me, I don't care how she goes, just as long as she bloody well does.

Enter TOM KETTLE, *wearing a heavy coat.*

CAITLIN. Morning, Tom Kettle.

UNCLE PAT. Morning, Tom. Is your roof still on?

TOM KETTLE. Aye, she's still on actually.

HONOR. Shena! Tom Kettle's here!

Enter SHENA *from upstairs.*

NUNU. Morning, Tom Kettle.

SHENA. Morning, Tom Kettle!

TOM KETTLE. Did you see the rainbow?

NUNU. What rainbow's that?

TOM KETTLE. This morning actually. I came over the ridge early, out for a walk. There she was. Must have been about half a mile high.

UNCLE PAT. Well, that's a grand start to any day. That's a good omen, so it is.

TOM KETTLE. Yeah. I collect rainbows actually.

UNCLE PAT. Do you now?

TOM KETTLE. Yeah. I've got a system actually.

UNCLE PAT. Do you now, Tom? And how does that work?

Pause.

TOM KETTLE. What?

UNCLE PAT. The rainbow system. How's that work now?

Beat.

TOM KETTLE. Right. Basically, when I see one, I make a notch on my front door there. I've got hundreds.

UNCLE PAT. Well, that's marvellous, Tom.

TOM KETTLE. Yeah. I've got different notches. In rows on the door there. Ninety-four snow, four hundred and forty-two thunder. Nineteen floods. And seven hundred and twelve rainbows. Seven hundred and thirteen.

TOM KETTLE *removes two apples from his pocket.*

Here I brung some windfalls actually.

Cheers from the GIRLS. *He takes out two more from the other pocket.*

They're from my own tree. I planted it myself.

He takes an apple out, then another. Then another. Then another. From both his pockets.

It's been a good year actually. What with that northerly blowing like it is.

I was collecting them half the morning. Dropping all around me they was. It was raining apples.

They all get several apples. Finally he pulls out a rabbit.

Hang about. Where did he spring from?

MERCY. Look at that!

HONOR. How does he do that?

SHENA. It's magic, so it is!

NUNU *takes the rabbit.*

What shall we call him?

HONOR. Lily!

SHENA. Sure, the last one was Lily.

CAITLIN. Tom Kettle, will you leave off with the rabbits. We've got dozens of the buggers in the lean-to there.

TOM KETTLE. Sorry, Caitlin. I forgot. You want an apple there, Oisin? I got a spare…

OISIN. No, Tom, you're grand.

They eat the apples.

CAITLIN. Quinn wants the tractor filled. But only half. He says the diesel tank needs filling.

TOM KETTLE. Right you are.

Enter MICHAEL CARNEY, *from down the stairs, doing up his dungarees.*

MICHAEL. Morning, Tom Kettle. Where's m'da?

CAITLIN. Out in the black barn. Killing the goose.

MICHAEL. I'm s'posed to be killing the goose!

CAITLIN. Not flat on your cracker in bed you're not. It's gone six.

AUNT PAT. Will you not keep it down! This is important, so it is.

MICHAEL *heads out*.

HONOR (*prompting her*). Aunt Cait…

CAITLIN. Stop right there, Michael Carney.

MICHAEL. What did I do?

CAITLIN. Honor here says you showed her your bumhole.

HONOR. It's Cleopatra.

MICHAEL. It was an accident.

CAITLIN. I see. And how's that?

MICHAEL. I was brushing my teeth. And… I dropped the toothpaste.

HONOR. Jesus, that's bollocks, so it is.

CAITLIN. Language, Cleopatra. (*To* MICHAEL.) Apologise please, Michael…

MICHAEL. Sorry, Cleopatra.

CAITLIN. Cleopatra, apologise to Jesus.

HONOR. Sorry, Jesus.

MICHAEL *shows* HONOR *crossed fingers. She sticks two up with her tongue out*.

Enter JJ.

JJ. Disaster has struck!

MERCY. What?

SHENA. What's happened?

JJ. The feckin' goose has escaped. Da went to the pen and the wee fecker's gone.

MICHAEL. It's in the black barn.

JJ. Not any more.

UNCLE PAT. Holy boots! How in the name of buggery did it get out?

JJ. Whoever fed the thing this morning left the latch on the pen open and it's got out and it's hightailed it. It's gone.

MERCY. The goose has gone? Oh Jesus! (*Bursts into tears.*)

NUNU. Mercy. Mercy. Mercy. This morning you were in floods 'cause it was gonna get done. Will you make up your bleedin' mind?

MERCY. But it's the harvest goose!

UNCLE PAT. I'm with the wean. This is a calamity.

JJ. Da's got the horse out…

CAITLIN. The horse?

MICHAEL. Wait there. I'll fire up the moped.

TOM KETTLE. She'll be down by the river. That's where I'd look.

MICHAEL (*searching a drawer*). Where are the damn keys to the moped?

MERCY. Can we come?

CAITLIN. You stay here and finish your kite.

MICHAEL (*finding the keys*). Got you, ya wee bastards. Let's go.

SHENA. Bagsy I go on the back of the moped!

Exeunt JJ, MICHAEL, SHENA, NUNU, *and* TOM KETTLE.

UNCLE PAT (*fixing himself another drink*). Well, that's the whole harvest shot clean to buggery right there. Big Jack'll be spinning in his grave, so he will.

AUNT PAT. Look on the bright side. At least it'll give you a half-decent story to tell. 'The Year the Goose Ran Off.' At least something *happens*. At least in that story the goose *actually* does something.

MERCY (*turning her apple core, by its stalk*). Uncle Pat. Why is Tom Kettle English?

UNCLE PAT. Because that's where he's from, Mercy. That's where he was born.

MERCY. I know that. What's he doing all the way out here?

UNCLE PAT. The short answer is nobody knows. Not even Tom Kettle. (*Beat.*) One summer eve long ago –

AUNT PAT. 'And we're off…'

UNCLE PAT. The wee'un has asked a perfectly good question. This is what being a family entails, Pat. The old ones passing on 'The Treasures of Yore' to the wee'uns. What else is the point in us still being here if not for that! It's what a family does, for Christ's sakes!

AUNT PAT. Tom Kettle is not family.

UNCLE PAT. For Jesus' sake, may I? Please? (*Beat.*) One summer evening, long ago, Big Jack was walking the land when he found a boy down by the river. Down by the mussel banks. Twelve years old.

AUNT PAT. Half-naked. Covered in shite.

UNCLE PAT. It's true to say when Big Jack found him he was somewhat dishevelled.

MERCY. But where did he come from?

UNCLE PAT. There are several theories. Perhaps his family were over from England, and they were in a crowded marketplace, or a fair, and he got lost. Or they were unsavoury types and he had the good sense to run away. The bottom line, it's a mystery.

AUNT PAT. Here's what happened. His mammy and daddy took one look at him at birth, realised they'd spawned a head-the-ball, got the boat over, took him off to the back of beyond, looked both ways, and shoved him off the feckin' train. His shirt came off, he rolled through fifteen types of shite, and pitched up here. If you ask me, his folks were smart. Quick shove in the back, you're shot of the wee beggar.

HONOR. But I thought Big Jack hated the English.

UNCLE PAT. That he did. To their marrow.

HONOR. Then why did he take one in?

MERCY. Right. Why didn't he just shoot him on sight?

AUNT PAT. That's an excellent point, Mercy.

UNCLE PAT. I think it speaks to Big Jack's kinder nature. Besides, I imagine it's not that easy in the course of an otherwise blissful sunny jaunt to stop off and summarily execute a destitute twelve-year-old boy.

AUNT PAT. Tell that to the Para who shot wee Sean McRory in front of his own mother. Tell it to Oliver Cromwell.

UNCLE PAT. Now, Pat. Let's not be teaching the wean that being English makes you wicked.

AUNT PAT. Well, girls, I'll say this. As a rule of thumb, it's proved uncannily accurate.

UNCLE PAT. Shakespeare. Wordsworth. William Blake.

AUNT PAT. William William William. Feckin' Billies to a man…

UNCLE PAT. I give up.

AUNT PAT. Balls, man. We're just getting started.

HONOR. Was Tom Kettle always… you know…

MERCY. Tap-tap curly-whirly cuckoo.

HONOR. Right. Was he always dead slow?

UNCLE PAT. I wouldn't say 'slow' so much as 'unhurried'. But you'd be surprised now. Old Tom Kettle has many talents.

AUNT PAT. Tom Kettle can't tie his shoelaces.

UNCLE PAT. Tom Kettle can put up a haystack in half an hour. Soon as the livestock hear his feet they start a chorus. Cows, calves, ewes, hens. His brains may be jitter-buggered, but with a hammer, a shovel, a diviner, Tom Kettle's your man. He's brung in thirty harvests for this family, so he has, while you've been sat there farting into that cushion.

CAITLIN *is laughing*.

AUNT PAT. Something funny, Caitlin?

CAITLIN. Nope. Everything's just as it should be, Aunt Pat.

The GIRLS *are giggling too.*

UNCLE PAT. Stop it. What did you hear me say?

HONOR. Nothing, Uncle Pat.

MERCY. Nothing, Uncle Pat.

Pause. AUNT PAT *is staring at* CAITLIN.

AUNT PAT. Well, it shows one thing. The Carneys always were a soft touch when it came to taking in strays.

CAITLIN *stops filling the kettle.*

CAITLIN. What was that, Aunt Pat?

AUNT PAT. I'm talking about the taking-in of strays, Caitlin.

Pause.

CAITLIN. Girls, go and get dressed now.

MERCY. Yes, Aunt Cait.

HONOR. Yes, Auntie Cait.

CAITLIN. Oisin, take that and finish it in the parlour. The stove's lit through there.

OISIN *leaves.*

Would you care to expand, Pat? Now it's just us here, and all?

AUNT PAT. Why, Caitlin, dear. You have me completely baffled, so you do. I was talking of Tom Kettle.

CAITLIN. Were you now.

AUNT PAT. A man who shares not a drop of Carney blood, who has no earthly reason to be here. Now why would you draw an affinity out of the thin air with a fella like him? Sure, it's baffling what the brain can build out of nothing, when it feels a certain way.

CAITLIN. You think you're light on your feet there, Pat? Still the sharp knife?

AUNT PAT. I assure you I was speaking only of Tom Kettle. (*Beat.*) And here's another name for you. Patsy O'Hara. Thomas McElwee.

UNCLE PAT. Can we not just have one day without this?

AUNT PAT. Kevin Lynch's body is buried fifteen miles from here. The North Wind blows over his grave, it'll be under that door in two minutes. The same wind, picking Tom Kettle's apples. There's boys in the H-blocks this morning too weak to lift a fork. While Tom Kettle's English belly is full. Who are we in a war with these past four hundred years? The Danish? The feckin' Franks? But don't worry because Tom Kettle can build you a haystack. He's a fine help come harvest time.

AUNT MAGGIE (*sings*).
    I heard the dogs howl in the moonlit night
    I went to the window to see the sight
    All the dead that I ever knew
    Going one by one and two by two...

UNCLE PAT. Are you all right there, Maggie?

CAITLIN. Are you right there, Aunt Maggie? Is there anything we can get you?

UNCLE PAT. You all right there, Mag? Would you like a cup of tea there?

AUNT MAGGIE. Pat, is that you?

UNCLE PAT (*brightening*). It's me, Maggie. It's Patrick...

AUNT MAGGIE. Is it harvest time, Pat?

UNCLE PAT (*beaming*). Indeed it is, Aunt Maggie. It's... it's absolutely harvest time! The Corcorans are coming. And there's a Harvest Breakfast, and a kite on the go, and a goose, possibly, and the men and the boys will be working night and day, and when it's over there's going to be a marvellous feast. Just like the old days.

AUNT MAGGIE. I can smell the barley.

UNCLE PAT. *There you go!* You get yourself a nice big lungful of that now.

AUNT MAGGIE. Is Daddy awake yet?

    Beat.

UNCLE PAT. No, Maggie. Big Jack's not here.

AUNT MAGGIE. Is he away?

UNCLE PAT. That's right, love. He's away now.

AUNT MAGGIE. Well, we can't start the harvest without Big Jack now. That's just not right. Besides, there's something I need to tell him... Something lovely that happened on the way home from school...

UNCLE PAT. Well, whatever it is, I'm sure he knows it.

AUNT MAGGIE *stares out, as if trying to remember.*

AUNT MAGGIE. Honestly, Maggie. What's got in to you? There in your fur collar and your knee-length swagger. You'll be fightin' 'em off down at McClaren's, so you will.

Pause.

UNCLE PAT. Maggie. Can you hear me, love?

AUNT MAGGIE (*sings*).
Where dips the rocky highland
Of Sleuth Wood in the lake,
There lies a leafy island
Where flapping herons wake
The drowsy water rats.
There we've hid our fairy vats
Full of berries
And of the reddest stolen cherries,
Come away, O, human child!
To the waters and the wild,
With a fairy hand in hand,
For the world's more full of weeping than you can
understand.

Silence.

UNCLE PAT. Are you comfortable, Maggie?

No answer.

Maggie?

Silence.

(*Brightly.*) Well, that wasn't bad. That wasn't bad at all.

CAITLIN. No it wasn't.

UNCLE PAT. She knows it's the harvest.

CAITLIN. She does.

UNCLE PAT (*excited*). Well, that's wonderful. How long's it been? And now look at her joining in like that. In the flow of the conversation. 'Morning, Pat!' she said. And you heard her.

CAITLIN. I did.

UNCLE PAT. And with the harvest. And and and… with the kite and all. And talking about the goose… And the barley. She's right there. She's right there now. Well, that's cheered me right up. That's cheered me right up, so it has. Holy boots. She said my name. You heard her say it.

CAITLIN. I did. I heard her say it loud and clear.

UNCLE PAT. Well, that's great, so it is. That's quite something.

Enter JJ, MICHAEL, SHENA and NUNU.

MICHAEL. EVERYBODY! LINE UP!

UNCLE PAT. Uh-oh. What's this?

Enter MERCY and HONOR from upstairs.

MERCY. What's happening?

HONOR. What is it, Michael?

MICHAEL. Don't ask questions, girl. Get in line.

Enter QUINN, through the boot room.

QUINN. A desperate situation has befallen us. For the first time in the history of this family, the harvest goose has done one. Now I don't have to tell you what a disaster this is. Not to mention the fact we've got the Corcoran boys on the bus from Derry as we speak, and we all know Shane Corcoran can eat two more spuds than a pig. (*Beat.*) So I want you to look deep into your souls. Deep now. And tell me. Which eejit left the door off the latch? Which drowsy, half-asleep turnip wandered out this morning, fed the bugger, and sauntered off leaving the pen wide open, allowing a painstakingly fattened fowl to wander off and begin life as one of God's wild creatures. Come on. Who's man enough to step forward?

OISIN (*off*). It was me.

   OISIN *walks out of the parlour, holding his kite. He stands there.*

   I fed the goose this morning. I must have left the latch off.

MICHAEL (*to* JJ). You owe me fifty pee.

JJ. Shh…

MICHAEL (*to* JJ). What did I say?

MERCY. Oisin, you daft eejit. We've been feeding that bugger night and day for months.

   QUINN *goes to* OISIN.

QUINN. Oisin Carney, do you have anything to say in your defence which might in any way mitigate the sentence due to be imposed.

OISIN. I just forgot, okay.

MICHAEL. He 'forgot'.

OISIN. Shut up, Michael.

MICHAEL. 'Earth to Planet Oisin. Come in, Oisin'…

JJ. Shut up, will ya…

OISIN. Why don't you get to fuck, Michael Carney?

CAITLIN. Oisin. Go to your room now.

OISIN. I don't want to play your stupid games. I'm not a child. Fuck the goose. And fuck you. You can all of youse go to hell.

   OISIN *smashes the kite on the kitchen table, tearing it with his hands. And runs out.*

QUINN. Oisin!

CAITLIN. Let him go.

   Silence.

MICHAEL. Well, that's grand. Grand sense of humour on your man.

JJ. You was winding him up.

MICHAEL. Jesus Christ, it was just a bit of fun... We always have a bit of a roar. It's tradition.

JJ. You knew what you were doing.

MICHAEL. There's no need to eat the bake off me. I was just having a laugh.

CAITLIN. Let him go. The boy's had a head a steam up all summer. I'll speak to him later.

HONOR *picks up the kite.*

HONOR. Why did he do that? That was our kite. He made it for us.

CAITLIN. He's just being daft is all.

Suddenly AUNT PAT *rises to her feet.*

AUNT PAT. Everybody. Stop what you're doing and listen. (*Loud.*) LISTEN TO THIS NOW!

AUNT PAT *marches forward and puts her transistor on the table. Turns it up full.*

MARGARET THATCHER (*on radio*). 'There can be no question of political status for someone who is serving a sentence for crime. Crime is crime is crime. It is not political. It is crime and there can be no question of granting political status. I just hope that anyone who is on hunger strike for his own sake will see fit to come off hunger strike, but that is a matter for him – '

QUINN *goes to the table and he switches the radio off.*

Pause.

AUNT PAT. What are you doing, man?

QUINN. There's a time and a place, Pat. It's not here, and it's not now.

AUNT PAT. Did you even hear what your woman there was saying?

QUINN. I don't care. This is my house. I'll ask you to respect that.

AUNT PAT. Did you not hear what she's calling us? Our very own Prime Minister. Her from over there. And she's calling *us* criminals! For what? For wanting feckin' shot of her.

QUINN. Pat –

AUNT PAT. For wanting our *own* to be our *own*. There's a time and a place all right. The time is NOW and the place is right feckin' here.

QUINN. Pat –

AUNT PAT bursts into tears. Shaking uncontrollably.

CAITLIN. Pat –

AUNT PAT. One after the other those poor lads have perished. And she did NOTHING! Now each night I get on my knees and I pray for the same thing. That that fuckin' bitch doesn't die in her sleep. If she was standing here I'd fuckin' take a knife from that drawer and I'd disembowel that smirking, sanctimonious, stone-hearted sow right here on this table, so I would. Then I'd show her what a fuckin' crime is…

QUINN. That's enough now.

AUNT PAT. '*A crime is a crime is a crime* – '

QUINN (*angry*). I SAID THAT'S ENOUGH.

Silence. AUNT PAT pulls herself together.

CAITLIN. Are you all right there, Aunt Pat?

Silence.

SHENA. Are you all right there, Aunt Pat?

AUNT PAT. I'm fine.

Silence.

CAITLIN. Aunt Pat. Do you need –

AUNT PAT. I SAID I'M FINE, CAITLIN. Thank you.

Silence.

AUNT PAT *goes to* AUNT MAGGIE, *and helps her up.*

Come on there, Maggie. Let's get you up there.

AUNT MAGGIE. Are we off now?

AUNT PAT. We're just going to get ourselves ready for the big day.

As she goes –

Sure, it seems there's some round here are a bit confused, so they are. Slowly, day by day, they're forgetting themselves. Forgetting where they are. Who they are.

She stops.

Have you forgotten your *own* history there, Quinn Carney? Good luck with that, is all I'll say. Good luck forgetting *that*.

Exit AUNT PAT *and* AUNT MAGGIE, *to the main house.*

Silence.

MICHAEL. Aunt Pat turning the air blue there.

UNCLE PAT. Ah, it's just the usual oul' toot. She's been at it since nineteen bloody sixteen so she has. She has to let it blow once in a while, or she'd explode, so she would. You watch. By lunchtime, she'll be right as rain.

HONOR. Are they really not eating nothing, Dad? The hunger strikers…

QUINN. They're not eating, Honor, no.

HONOR. Not even biscuits?

QUINN. Not biscuits, no.

HONOR. But if I don't eat I get fuzzy. Angry too. Like I want to punch something.

MERCY. Are you allowed a cup of tea? Or squash?

SHENA. Perhaps Aunt Pat's right. Perhaps it's wrong.

UNCLE PAT. Now now, Shena –

HONOR. Maybe that's why the goose has done one. Maybe it's a sign.

MARY. Is everything all right?

They all stop, and look up to the top of the stairs.

MARY CARNEY *stands there.*

UNCLE PAT. Mary. You're up.

She walks down the stairs.

SHENA. Are you feeling better, Ma?

NUNU. Ma. Are you all right? How is your virus?

MARY. Thank you, Nunu. I'm feeling a bit better. But I'd love a cup of tea.

NUNU. Coming right up.

QUINN. Are you all right there, love?

MARY. I slept a bit.

He gives her a quick hug and a peck.

I heard shouting.

UNCLE PAT. Oh, that. That was nothing. Have a seat, Mary.

He winks. Then goes to fix himself a drink.

QUINN. Have a seat there, lass…

MARY. Caitlin, the baby is crying up there. Would you go up and see if you can get him to sleep?

CAITLIN. Certainly, Mary.

CAITLIN *goes upstairs.*

MARY. So how's the morning so far? Some shouting, is that all…?

SHENA. Just the usual, Ma… (*Kisses her.*)

MICHAEL. Yeah… Nothing special.

UNCLE PAT. To give you a quick recap there, Mary, just to fill you in on the morning's activities, on what you've missed – I've had a lovely shave, Tom Kettle saw a rainbow, Cleopatra has sunk a whole bottle of vitamin-C tablets, the goose has done one, Mrs Thatcher called us a bunch of criminals and Oisin banjaxed the kite. Otherwise it's been fairly peaceful, wouldn't you say? Otherwise all's well in the world.

UNCLE PAT *is pouring himself another.*

Well, I think it's time for a wee pick-me-up. A tonic for the troops.

MARY. None for me, thank you. I'm only just upright.

UNCLE PAT. Well, the boys can have a wee nip, surely?

QUINN. Half a thimbleful…

MICHAEL. Ah, come on, Da…

QUINN. Under-tens half a thimbleful. Over-tens a thimbleful. No more.

General cheers.

UNCLE PAT. That's the spirit! Get some glasses, Shena.

As UNCLE PAT *pours them all a drink, he sings the first two lines of the second chorus of 'An Irish Harvest Day' by Michael Maloney. Everyone joins in and sings the rest of the chorus together.*

During the song, HORRIGAN *enters into the boot room. He waits on the threshold.*

Who shall we toast?

MICHAEL. Margaret Thatcher!

JJ. Elvis Presley!

ALL. CLEOPATRA! / DAVID BOWIE! / LIAM BRADY! / MISS PIGGY! / THE HUMAN LEAGUE! / FATHER CHRISTMAS! / *TOP OF THE POPS!!*

UNCLE PAT. To Mary and Quinn. Mary, a fine woman, mother of seven wonderful children, a beautiful wife, and to Quinn, the only bugger lucky enough to win her heart.

ALL. To Mary and Quinn… / To Mum and Dad.

They all drink.

JJ. That's beezer, so it is…

MICHAEL. First of many.

QUINN. Go easy. We got a long day ahead.

MERCY. I'm drunk! I'm drunk!

MARY. Honestly, Pat, what have you done to these children?

Enter HORRIGAN.

HORRIGAN. Good morning.

Everyone reacts. Calms down, etc.

MARY. Father. Welcome.

ALL. Good morning. / Morning, Father…

HORRIGAN. Good morning, all. Good morning, Patrick. Girls. Good morning, Michael. I hope I'm not interrupting.

QUINN. No. Not at all. Come in, Father. Would you like a cup of tea there, Father?

HORRIGAN. Thank you, Quinn. I won't. I can't stay too long.

MARY. Put those glasses away, children…

Pause.

UNCLE PAT. So what is it, Father? Have you come get a bead on? Sleeves up, shoulder to the wheel. Has the clergy finally come to *earn* its tithe, now?

HORRIGAN. Oh, I think I'm a ways past bailing, Pat.

UNCLE PAT. Well, you know what they say. It's never too late to pull a muscle.

HORRIGAN (*tries to smile*). Tell me, Mary. Is young Caitlin about?

QUINN. She's upstairs. With the baby.

HORRIGAN. Right. It's just I need to speak to her.

MARY. She'll be down in just a minute.

QUINN. Is everything okay, Father?

Beat.

HORRIGAN. Thank you, Quinn. I'm fine.

MICHAEL. You know I'm glad you came over, Father, because there's something extremely important I have to tell you. (*Beat*.) So your man Father O'Mulligan is down in County Cork, and he's doing his rounds, and the rain's lashing down.

MARY. Oh, Michael, honestly –

MICHAEL. So he comes to the first house, and Mrs Murphy says, 'Oh, Father, you must be frozen, have a nice hot cup of tea.' 'No tea,' says Father O'Mulligan, and gave them his blessing and went on his way. So he comes to the second house –

HORRIGAN. I'm going to have to stop you there I'm afraid, Michael. (*Beat*.) I'd love to hear your joke but it'll have to be saved for another time.

MICHAEL *looks at the others. Embarrassed*.

I do need to speak to Caitlin. But thinking about it now, I think first I need to speak to you, Quinn.

Beat.

QUINN. Sure, Father.

HORRIGAN. Is there somewhere we could have a private word?

QUINN. Of course, Father. We can go in the wee office there…

NUNU. The parlour's roasting, Dad.

QUINN. Right enough.

MARY. You sure you wouldn't like a cup of tea first, Father?

HORRIGAN. No thank you, Mary.

QUINN (*re: the parlour*). This way, Father…

Exit QUINN *and* HORRIGAN *into the parlour. Pause*.

MICHAEL (*sarcastic*). Nah, you're dead-on there, Father. Just cut me off at the knees any time you like.

MARY. Don't be rude, Michael.

MICHAEL. I was halfway through a joke, so I was. You don't cut a man off when he's mid-joke. It's practically illegal.

SHENA. You went bright red.

MICHAEL. Too bloody right I did. Swallow-me-up moment, so it was. What if on Sunday when he's halfway through his sermon, and I spring up and said, 'Here, Father! Father Horrigan! Is it all right if I pop to the jacks?' How do you think he'd feel?

MERCY. What does Father Horrigan want, Ma?

MARY. We don't know, Mercy.

UNCLE PAT *pours himself another.*

UNCLE PAT. Sure, it's been a strange half an hour so it has. Very, very strange indeed.

Enter TOM KETTLE, *covered in mud, with a live goose under his arm.*

Everybody stops.

JJ. Jesus Christ. Will you look at that now.

MICHAEL. That's him! That's the very fella!

SHENA. Where was he?

TOM KETTLE. Down by the river.

CAITLIN *comes back downstairs.*

CAITLIN. Jeez. Is that not our very own Tom Kettle saving the day there?

MICHAEL. How did you catch her?

JJ. What happened?

TOM KETTLE. She was down by the river. I thought, 'She's down by the river.' So I went down by the river.

Beat.

JJ. Okay. So we've established she was down by the river. What happened next?

TOM KETTLE. I saw a kingfisher.

MICHAEL. Okay, let's focus here, Tom. Let's stay on task. What happened next with the *goose*?

Beat.

TOM KETTLE. So I crept up but she saw me coming. She crossed over, but I waded after her and then she made a dash for it across that marshland there towards the road, but I come round her blind side and cut her off.

UNCLE PAT. What was I saying? What was I just saying about hidden talents? There's not many a man could chase and bring to ground a wild goose across choppy bogland in just a pair of welly boots. That takes qualities, so it does. Rare, rare qualities.

MICHAEL. Well, what are we waiting for? Let's get her in the black barn and wring her neck.

HONOR. Can I watch?

MERCY. Me too.

HONOR *and* MERCY. Please, Ma. Please!!

MARY. Jeez, but you're a bloodthirsty wee pair. Get your coats on.

HONOR *and* MERCY. Yes! / Hooray!

TOM KETTLE. Come on then. If you're quick. Bye, Mrs Carney.

MARY. Bye, Tom.

Exit TOM KETTLE (*with the goose*), HONOR, MERCY, SHENA *and* NUNU.

JJ. Okay. That's it. I'm not waiting round for the old man all bloody day. Michael John Patrick Carney!

MICHAEL *leaps up.*

MICHAEL (*American accent*). Sir yes sir?

JJ. I want all the troops in the yard in one minute. Take the big girls and the tractor up on Dunn's ground. Me and Uncle Pat on the combine.

MICHAEL. Sir yes sir!

Exit MICHAEL, JJ, NUNU, *and* UNCLE PAT.

CAITLIN. Michael. Don't forget to fill the tractor…!

MICHAEL (*off*). Right y'are.

CAITLIN *and* MARY *are alone.* MARY *at the table.*

CAITLIN *clears up the broken kite. Puts it in the bin.*

CAITLIN. Well, that's a bit more like it now.

MARY. Is the baby sleeping?

CAITLIN. He is. I gave him a wee feed he went straight down.

MARY. There now.

CAITLIN *busies herself with some drying and a rack.*

MARY *reaches forward and switches on the radio. Finds some classical music. Switches it off.*

Silence.

CAITLIN. I'm glad you're feeling more yourself there, Mary.

MARY. I am, thank you. It feels like I've turned the corner there.

CAITLIN. That's good.

Silence.

Did I not see Father Horrigan's car pulling up out there?

MARY. You did indeed. He's in the parlour there, talking to Quinn. Some or other business.

CAITLIN. Right.

Silence.

Enter AUNT PAT. *There's a sense of relief in* MARY *that they are no longer alone. Perhaps in* CAITLIN *too.*

MARY. Well, don't you look a picture, Pat?

AUNT PAT. I saw the Father's car out the bathroom window there. So I made myself presentable.

MARY. Well, you look lovely. Doesn't she look lovely, Cait?

CAITLIN. Aye, she does.

AUNT PAT *sits at the table.*

AUNT PAT. There now.

Pause.

Jim Joe's got them all mustering out in the yard there. It's strange seeing him taking the reins like that. Seems like only two harvests back they were all running round in nappies.

MARY. Aye, it does, Pat. You look up and ten years have flown past. Are you looking forward to seeing the Corcorans?

AUNT PAT. Aye, it'll be grand, I'm sure. The whole family together, round the same table.

MARY. Aye. It's a precious thing.

CAITLIN. It is.

Pause.

AUNT PAT. You know, looking out the window and seeing the Father's car there reminded me of a funny story. Do you remember when you were last poorly, Mary, we had a visit from the Father, and he brought with him an old friend from his seminary days. Do you remember, Caitlin? His name was Father Connolly. You were upstairs there, Mary, and we were all down here, and we had a wonderful meal, all the children there, and Caitlin cooked the most delicious pie. I'll never forget it. It was absolutely perfect in every way. And the littlest ones were dancing. And Quinn was joking, and Michael was telling jokes, and there was laughter all round. And at the end of it all, Father Connolly turned to Caitlin and said, 'Mrs Carney, your children are all wonderful, so they are.'

Pause.

Can you imagine? All the way through that meal, two hours of conversation and all the time thinking that Quinn and Caitlin were man and wife. And that all *your* wee ones were *their* wee ones. When he learned the truth he was mortified, so he was. He went red as an apple. Now can you imagine walking in here and misreading the situation so completely? Sure, he must have had a glass or two to make a crashing blunder like that.

Pause.

MARY. Well, that's a funny story, Pat. A very funny story. I'll have to try and remember it.

AUNT PAT. But the thing I remember most about that afternoon wasn't the old man's blunder. It was that pie. It was so succulent. It's making my mouth water just to recall it.

Silence.

Enter QUINN *from the parlour.*

QUINN. I need to speak to Caitlin alone.

MARY. What's wrong?

QUINN. I just need five minutes here.

MARY. I'll take this tea upstairs.

MARY *leaves.*

AUNT PAT *looks at them both.*

AUNT PAT. Well, now. We'll leave you two alone then.

She gets up. Leaves.

QUINN *and* CAITLIN *are all alone.*

CAITLIN. What's wrong?

Pause.

QUINN. They've found Seamus.

Pause.

CAITLIN. Where?

QUINN. In a bog across the border.

Silence.

Slowly she nods. Then begins to shake. He comes to her and hugs her.

CAITLIN. It's okay. It's okay.

They break. Silence.

QUINN. Sit down.

CAITLIN. I'm okay.

QUINN. Sit down there, now.

CAITLIN. I don't want to sit down.

QUINN. Do as you're told.

She does. He fetches her a glass. Fills it with whiskey. She drinks it. He refills it.

Silence.

CAITLIN. Where did they find him?

QUINN. Over the border there.

CAITLIN. Where?

QUINN. I don't know. The Father told me but I wasn't fucking listening.

CAITLIN. How long has he been there?

QUINN. The whole time.

She drinks. Nods.

CAITLIN. Well, they've made a mistake.

QUINN. Cait –

CAITLIN. Three years after Seamus vanished, Gerry McKee came to me in the playground by St Leonards and told me he'd seen Seamus on the ferry over from Dublin to Wales. He said he was playing the slot machines and Gerry went up and had a wee chat.

QUINN. Cait –

CAITLIN. Hang on, because I've got this memorised. In May 1976, Seamus is seen at a petrol station in Carrickfergus. Filling up a minibus –

QUINN. They have his body. They've checked his dental records.

CAITLIN. Well, they should check them again. Two years ago your man Tommy O'Brien stops me in the Spar, says he saw my Seamus in a pub in Liverpool. (*Stops*.) No, it was longer than that. I'm getting confused. I was stood there at the checkout, and I was there and Oisin was there, I had him next to me, and –

She stops.

QUINN. He had a picture of Oisin. And this…

He gives her an envelope. She opens it. It's his wedding ring. She looks at it.

Silence.

CAITLIN. Do you have a smoke there?

QUINN. Course.

He rolls her a cigarette. Silence. She starts to cry.

CAITLIN. How did they do it?

QUINN. Cait –

CAITLIN. I want to know.

Pause.

QUINN. He was shot in the head.

Silence.

CAITLIN. Where did you say?

QUINN. County Louth.

Pause.

The Father's in there. He has all the information.

CAITLIN. I just want to sit here for a moment.

He gives her the cigarette. Lights it. She inhales. Breathes out smoke. Silence.

(*Re: wedding ring*.) Well, at least I can stop paying this off now.

QUINN. Aye, you can.

Pause.

CAITLIN. We'd had a fight. The night before. I can't even remember what. He slept downstairs on the couch there. The morning he left, he never said goodbye. He goes off to work…

She puts the ring back in the envelope and tosses it on the table. Finishes her drink.

Look at me. The Corcorans are going to show up and I'm gonna have a bake like a fucking beachball, so I am.

QUINN. I'll send 'em home.

CAITLIN. There's the pack lunches to make… What? Don't be stupid. There's crop to bring in.

QUINN. The crop can stand another week.

CAITLIN. Don't be fuckin' daft, Quinn.

QUINN. Cait –

CAITLIN. No. Under no circumstances. I've waited ten years. What's one more day?

QUINN. Cait –

CAITLIN. I'm serious. Or I'm gonna fuckin' explode, so I am. We don't tell anyone. The harvest comes and goes, and tomorrow… Tomorrow we'll tell them. Christ, after ten years, what's one more day? I'm not having those bastards wreck ten years *and* a fuckin' party.

Pause.

QUINN. Are you sure?

CAITLIN. What? Yes. I'm sure.

QUINN. Then okay.

Pause.

CAITLIN. I'm fuckin' wrecked so I am.

QUINN *takes the whiskey. Takes a swig. Holds it up.*

QUINN. To Seamus Carney.

CAITLIN. To him an' all. The fuckin' wee prick. (*Swigs.*)

Silence.

I'm going to find Oisin...

QUINN. Are you going to tell him?

CAITLIN. No. I just want to... I just want to hold him.

QUINN. Look up on the Ridge. He sometimes goes up there.

CAITLIN. I'll find him. I'll tell him tomorrow. Tomorrow.

She leaves.

QUINN *sits alone.*

We see OISIN *has been listening.*

Silence.

Enter HORRIGAN.

HORRIGAN. You'll be wanting the funeral here, I'm guessing. What I'm saying is, I'd be proud to administer, organise the necessary, and see Seamus on his way.

QUINN. Who called you?

Beat.

HORRIGAN. What?

QUINN. Who told you he'd been found?

HORRIGAN. Quinn, listen, I appreciate this is a huge shock and all, even after all this time. Especially after all this time...

QUINN. Why are you not answering my question, Father?

HORRIGAN. No, I'll... What... No. I'll answer it... What was it... Yesterday it was, I was asked to come into Derry –

QUINN. Who asked you to go there...? Who did you meet?

HORRIGAN. Quinn –

QUINN. Listen to me now, Father. Who specifically did you meet? Who did you sit in front of, and talk to. Whose face were you looking at...

HORRIGAN. For Christ's sake, Quinn.

QUINN. If you ever loved this family, tell me the truth now. On your soul. On Seamus Carney's immortal soul, who was it?

HORRIGAN. I can't remember.

Pause.

QUINN. Thank you for coming here today. Now I have to ask you to leave.

HORRIGAN. Quinn –

QUINN. It's not your fault. You've been a rock for this family. But you must leave now.

HORRIGAN. I'm so sorry.

QUINN. It's not your fault. But you have to go.

HORRIGAN. Quinn –

QUINN. Leave this house, Father. You've done all you can.

HORRIGAN *goes to the door. Stops.*

HORRIGAN. He's going to come here. He's not finished with you. I looked him in the eye.

Silence.

God be with you, Quinn Carney.

HORRIGAN *leaves.*

QUINN *stands alone.*

JJ *enters.*

JJ. Dad, the Corcorans have arrived. Are you coming or what?

QUINN. Aye, I'll be there.

JJ. Well, come on, man! It's harvest time!

JJ *runs back outside.*

Alone, QUINN *pours himself a whiskey. Downs it. He heads out into the yard.*

Sounds from out in the yard. Whoops, as the CORCORANS *are welcomed.*

An engine starting.

OISIN *comes out of the parlour. He's been listening.*

He stands there, uncertain of what to do.

Enter TOM KETTLE, *with the dead goose over his shoulder.*

OISIN *hides.*

TOM KETTLE *hangs the goose up above the sink. And leaves out to the yard.*

Slowly, OISIN *comes back out of the shadows.*

He stands there, alone, staring at the dead goose, hanging there.

Blackout.

End of Act One.

ACT TWO

Music.

In darkness, a baby, crying.

Light.

The farmhouse kitchen. One minute before sunset. The room is empty, except for AUNT MAGGIE, *sitting alone.*

And in the middle of the table, the baby, naked, crying.

Enter SHENA, *with a safety pin and a towelling nappy, and a bundle of clothes. As she dresses the baby she sings the first verse and chorus of 'Kids in America' by Marty Wilde and Ricky Wilde.*

The sounds of the harvest in the distance.

SHENA. Can you hear that? That's the old combine. That's Daddy out there, he's got all his sons and the Corcoran boys. There's big handsome Shane and wee Diarmaid. And young Declan with the boils on his back. They're all out there, in the dust and the dapple and the sweat. Some day you'll be out there with them. A Carney boy. With those big strong arms of yours. With your big strong daddy looking on. Aye, Daddy's in the field, soldier. Doing his duty. And your mummy? She's upstairs resting like a lazy bitch. That's right, poppet. She's got another virus. And so has my arse. She calls it a virus but we know she's always got a fecking virus. She never gets up, does she? Just lies around scoffing custard creams, filing her bunions, brewing some fucking Scotch-mist ailment or other while we do all the work. Is that nice and snug now? *There.*

She sings the first few lines of the last verse.

AUNT MAGGIE. Hello, Shena.

SHENA *almost drops the baby.*

54

SHENA. Jesus Christ, Aunt Maggie. You scared the shite out of me.

AUNT MAGGIE. Are the men still out?

SHENA. They'll be back any minute.

AUNT MAGGIE. I watched the sun going down just now, and the light creep across the flags there. The harvest is in. And the night has come, and it's time for the feast.

Silence.

SHENA *runs out.*

SHENA (*off*). Everyone, come quick. Aunt Maggie Faraway is back!

Re-enter SHENA (*with the baby*), *followed by* NUNU, MERCY *and* HONOR.

HONOR. Aunt Maggie Faraway!

NUNU. Where have you been, Aunt Maggie Faraway?

MERCY. Aunt Maggie, Aunt Maggie!

ALL. Tell us, Aunt Maggie! Where did you travel to? / Tell us! Tell us!

AUNT MAGGIE. This time, my darlings, your Great-Aunt Maggie has been south, to the Mountains of Cork.

NUNU. What century?

AUNT MAGGIE. The nineteenth.

MERCY. What year?

AUNT MAGGIE. 1802. February 19th to be precise. The eve of the great faerie battle between the Fir Bolgs and the Tanuth Dé!

NUNU. I love this one! It's so violent!

SHENA. Ssh, Nunu. Go on, Aunt Maggie.

AUNT MAGGIE. Now, the Fir Bolgs were Fierce Faeries, warmongers, who said the land belonged only to them. The Tanuth Dé King, Nuada, asked that they be given half the island, but the Fir Bolg King refused. So the two sides met last Tuesday at the Pass of Balgatan. During the battle, Sreng, fierce champion of the Fir Bolg, called out, 'Nuada, I challenge thee to single combat.' The field fell silent. Nuada stared Sreng straight in the eye and said, 'Drop dead, ya wee prick. And feck off while you're doing it.' This turned out to be a massive tactical error. With one sweep of his sword, Sreng cut off Nuada's right hand –

HONOR. His left hand –

ALL. His ears! His nose!

AUNT MAGGIE. And then his head! However, the brave Fir Bolg were defeated and their King slain. The Fir Bolg were just deciding how to get revenge, when I heard the sound of the old combine out there on the breeze, and saw the light on the flags, and I was home again…

NUNU. Quick. Let's ask questions.

HONOR. How many children will I have?

AUNT MAGGIE. Honor Carney, you'll have four boys and five girls. And the youngest will be born on Christmas Day and she shall be double-jointed.

NUNU. What about me, Aunt Maggie?

AUNT MAGGIE. You, Nunu. You'll have twins, twice. All redhead boys. All born in the summer.

MERCY. What about Shena?

SHENA. You can leave me out of this. I don't want none of the feckers. Soon as I turn sixteen I'm off to London to marry Adam Ant. Isn't that right, Aunt Maggie?

NUNU. Ask her another question. A proper one.

MERCY. Does Shane Corcoran fancy our Shena?

SHENA. Who's going to win the Eurovision Song Contest?

HONOR. Why didn't *you* have any children, Aunt Maggie?

Pause.

NUNU. Aunt Maggie?

MERCY. Maybe she doesn't want to say.

AUNT MAGGIE. No, I'll answer. The truth, girls. The truth is…
I loved a man who loved another. He was from Killborren. His
name was Francis John Patrick Maloney. The son of a house
painter. All the boys from our village were small and pasty and
dark, or bright ginger goblins with blue skin and clammy
hands, like deep-sea fish, but shyer. But Francis Maloney…
Francis had a long strong back and golden hair. Bronzed skin.
And green eyes. Like a minor river god. Like Morrigan sprung
to life in Kilborren. From the age of ten, whenever I spied
Francis I was struck cross-eyed with lust. My mouth went dry.
My heart sped to bursting. I'd lie awake at night dreaming of
us being together, going swimming together in the river, lying
on the bank after, in the long daisies. And then one day
packing up all the small things we owned and sailing off to
America to live in New York, ride the subway with our ten
fair-haired, green-eyed boys and girls. Tuck them to bed and
sit up at a rickety table with one candle, drinking bourbon and
branch water, reading each other Whitman, Thoreau, Emily
Dickinson. Then blow out the candle, climb into our crisp cold
cot and make that old contraption roar and rumble like a
Rolls-Royce Silver Shadow at full feckin' pelt. When I was
fifteen years old, I woke up one morning and my mammy told
me Francis had moved away, across the water there to
England, to help the English dig their canal from Birmingham
to Coventry. I waited years for him to return. Then one day
I heard he'd married a girl from the Black Country there, over
in England. A seamstress. And it broke my heart. (*Beat.*) I've
lived a happy life, but Love… Love had happened for me.
And the funny thing was… I'm not sure Francis Maloney ever
knew I existed. No more than any other soppy girl he passed
in the street. But for me… it was Love. And so it never
seemed fair to take another, and be with him, and bear his
children, when all the time my heart would be away. But I'll
never forget the feeling of seeing Francis, seventeen years old,
in church, his glorious golden neck diving into a starch-white
collar, throwing back his mane, singing 'Be Thou My Vision'.
I swear to Christ I could have ridden that boy from here to
Connemara. And back.

HONOR. Auntie Maggie!

SHENA. Jeez… That's fuckin' priceless.

MERCY. Quick, ask her another.

SHENA. I've got one. Why is Aunt Pat such an old bitch?

NUNU. Shena!

MERCY. Shena, shame on you.

SHENA. Hang about. I bet she knows the answer.

Pause.

AUNT MAGGIE. Well, Shena, your Aunt Pat has lived a very difficult life. It's not easy being the oldest.

SHENA. Tell me about it.

AUNT MAGGIE. Except, see, Aunt Pat wasn't always the oldest. There was Michael John. Michael was born on the last day of the last month of the last year of the last century. New Year's Eve, 1899. From the get, he was a handful. When he was seven he was leader of a gang twice his age. He'd fight you all day for a conker. Sharp as a needle and funny as all shite. He was Pat's hero. She *worshipped* him. Something in Michael rang Pat's bell and it's still ringing to this day. You see, girls, you couldn't make Michael do anything he didn't feel in his heart was right. You couldn't get him in a corner, or take what was his. *And he'd never turn his back on you, no matter what.* It was in his blood.

Pause.

When he was fifteen, Michael joined the Irish Republican Brotherhood. He left this farm and walked from here to Dublin, scrumping apples all the way. Pat was heartbroken. She wrote Michael letters, but got no reply. It was then Pat started to learn about the Brotherhood. About Ireland. And about the English. She spent all winter up in her room, reading by candlelight. She learned the lot. Oliver Cromwell. Daniel O'Connell, Charles Stuart Parnell. And when the spring came, she wrote to Michael, a long letter of love, almost fifty pages, filled with everything she'd learned. And he sent back one piece of paper. A hand-drawn map, showing all the best apple orchards between Armagh and Dublin.

Pause.

She never even said goodbye. She walked south. She arrived in Dublin one sunny morning in April, 1916. 22nd April. Two days before the Easter Rising.

Pause.

Pat looked everywhere for Michael but she couldn't find him. He'd left his room, he was already at action stations. When the fighting started, Michael found himself with all the others holed up in the GPO with Patrick Pearce. James Connolly, the O'Rahilly. On the Thursday, Michael and the O'Rahilly led the charge out of the GPO, into the maw of the English machine guns. He managed to escape, but he was wounded in the groin. Completely by chance, Pat found him bleeding in the street. Bleeding out. He looked at her and he said, 'Pat, love, I clean forgot it was Easter. And there'd be no feckin' apples on the trees. Sure, girl, you must be starving.' She took her handkerchief and tried to staunch the blood, but there was too much of it. Right before he died he looked her in the eye, and he gave her his pistol. And he smiled and said, 'Death to the English, Pat.' And Pat wrapped the pistol in the bloody handkerchief.

Pause.

A month after the Rising I came home from school and I found the back door of the house wide open. And I went out, and out there behind our house, was my big sister. Standing out in the field, holding Michael's pistol. All alone.

Pause.

Except she wasn't alone. There were others in the field with her. They were the *Banshees*. Ten thousand. Banshees from Fermanagh, Tyrone, Derry, Antrim, Down, Armagh, Wexford, Dublin, Donegal, Sligo, Galway, Limerick. Everywhere. And they were all screaming. Screaming in unison. Screaming and pointing at the sky.

Silence.

SHENA. Aunt Maggie?

NUNU. Aunt Maggie?

Silence.

HONOR. Aunt Maggie. Did my dad ever kill a man?

SHENA. Honor –

HONOR. I want to know.

Pause.

Is he a killer, Aunt Maggie?

Pause.

NUNU. Aunt Maggie? What happened to Uncle Seamus?

AUNT MAGGIE. Seamus is in the ground, girls. Seamus is in the ground.

Silence.

SHENA. Aunt Maggie.

NUNU. Aunt Maggie.

MERCY. Aunt Maggie…

Pause.

NUNU. She's gone again.

Pause.

MERCY. Goodbye, Aunt Maggie. We love you.

NUNU. We love you, Aunt Maggie. Safe travels.

MERCY. I love it when she visits. But it's so sad when she goes.

Pause.

NUNU. Jaysus fucking Christ.

MERCY. Jesus. What do we tell Aunt Cait?

SHENA. Nothing.

MERCY. But she said Seamus is in the ground.

SHENA. Sure, half of what Aunt Maggie says comes with a pinch of salt.

NUNU. But we have to tell her!

MERCY. Yes, we have to!

SHENA. Is that so, Mercy? Who showed Dan Doyle her knickers? (*To* NUNU.) Who's got a pack of Woodbine stuffed in her satchel?

NUNU. I won't breathe a word.

MERCY. Me either.

SHENA. Good. Well, that's that.

Pause.

HONOR. Nine kids. Fuck me blue.

NUNU. What about two sets of feckin' twins? How the hell am I going to manage that?

MERCY. Here. Where'd'you suppose it is?

NUNU. What?

MERCY. The pistol. The gun. Michael's shooter. There's no way she hasn't still got it.

NUNU. Search me.

SHENA. She probably keeps it in her hole.

MERCY (*to* HONOR). What are you doing, asking her about Dad?

HONOR. Because I want to know.

MERCY. Well, tough luck.

Enter CAITLIN, *into the porch.*

NUNU. Someone's coming.

SHENA. Sssshh…

CAITLIN *comes in.*

HONOR. Aunt Cait!

MERCY. Auntie Cait!

HONOR. We just had a visit. From Aunt Maggie Faraway.

NUNU. A massive one.

CAITLIN goes to the cupboard and pours herself a large drink. Drinks it in one.

CAITLIN. What did I miss?

Pause.

SHENA. Honor's going to have nine babies. And I'm going to marry Adam Ant.

HONOR. She never said that. She never said nothing about Adam Ant.

MERCY. She told a sad story. About how she was in love with a man she couldn't have. And he never knew.

NUNU. Francis Maloney.

HONOR. He never even knew she existed.

MERCY. She spent her whole life in love with him. But he was married over there in England. She never loved another. Can you imagine, Aunt Cait? All those years with a burning love and nowhere for it to grow.

CAITLIN. Is the baby in bed?

SHENA. I was just taking him. Then Aunt Maggie started telling the story –

CAITLIN (*sternly*). Well, do it now, please. Mercy and Honor. Get changed.

MERCY. But they're not back.

HONOR. They're still in the field.

CAITLIN. Do it now, please, girls.

SHENA. Yes, Aunt Cait.

HONOR. Yes, Aunt Cait. Come on, Mercy.

The GIRLS leave.

CAITLIN *takes the goose out of the oven.*

Silence.

CAITLIN. What shall I do, Aunt Maggie?

Pause.

Aunt Maggie. Please help me.

She goes over, and kneels and holds AUNT MAGGIE'*s hands.*

Help me, Aunt Maggie. Please. Help me. What should I do?

Enter QUINN.

CAITLIN *stands. Busies herself.*

Where are the others? Are they not down yet?

QUINN. Have you slept?

CAITLIN (*calls*). Girls. Your father's here.

QUINN. Cait –

CAITLIN. Is Oisin with you?

QUINN. He's with the others.

CAITLIN. That's grand. Go and get washed up now.

QUINN. Have you slept?

CAITLIN. I said I'm fine...

QUINN. Are you sure?

Beat.

CAITLIN. I'm fuckin' steaming.

QUINN. We don't have to do this.

CAITLIN. No. We agreed.

QUINN. Cait –

CAITLIN. No. The Corcorans have come a long way. I'm not ruining the whole day...

QUINN. Cait –

CAITLIN. I won't have it. I won't let them. I won't let them. (*Beat*.) In the morning. We'll tell him. We'll tell everyone. One more night, that's all I want. Just one.

He looks at her.

QUINN. One night.

Noise from outside.

Exit QUINN.

We hear all the CARNEY BOYS *and the* CORCORANS. *Everyone sings the first verse and refrain of 'Monto (Take Her Up to Monto)' by George Desmond Hodnett.*

The porch door opens.

MICHAEL. Christ. I need a drink!

JJ. I need three!

Enter MICHAEL, JJ, DIARMAID CORCORAN, SHANE CORCORAN *and* DECLAN CORCORAN. *All dirty, dusty. Queueing up to drink from the water tap. Passing a whiskey bottle.*

JJ *sings the first three lines of the second verse.* MICHAEL *sings the next three and then everyone else joins in to sing the refrain.*

CAITLIN. Sit down, boys. It's on the turn.

Enter UNCLE PAT, *hopping, his arm round* TOM KETTLE.

What happened?

UNCLE PAT. Nothing happened. I may have stumbled on the way down.

MICHAEL. Arse over tit is more like it.

Laughter.

SHANE (*simultaneous*). There you go now!

DIARMAID (*simultaneous*). That's the way, big man…!

TOM KETTLE. Evening, Caitlin. You look very nice.

MICHAEL. Aunt Cait, you look beautiful. Seriously. You look a treasure.

CAITLIN. Give me that.

She takes the bottle from him.

Sit.

MICHAEL. Here, Aunt Cait. Declan nearly got dragged through the bailer.

DECLAN. I did not.

MICHAEL. We're on Dunn's Ground, bailing up, it's all going fine when the fecker stalls. This one, sticks his bake in the hot end, he's poking round and then he says, 'Switch her on.'

DIARMAID. Eeejit…

DECLAN. Bull. My bake –

MICHAEL. Listen now…

DECLAN. My beauty was never in danger. Never in danger.

MICHAEL. Then JJ fires whole thing up – (*Makes noise of harvester.*) and Declan sticks his head up with this look on his face like –

MICHAEL does an impersonation. The others all crack up, as CAITLIN puts the goose on the table and begins to carve.

I'm telling you, Cait. You had to be there.

JJ. Careful, bro. You'll be making these townmice think we don't know what we're doing.

SHANE. You don't know what you're doing.

Jeers.

Well, if you ask me the star of the show was Young O…

MICHAEL. The Big O. (*Bangs the table.*) Fourteen summers young, and he hauled bails with the best of them. Ten straight hours. No tears. No crying for his mammy *at all*.

OISIN (*shy, but pleased*). Ah, piss off, Michael.

MICHAEL. To Oisin Carney. One of the best.

ALL. One of the best. / Oisin Carney.

MICHAEL. I'll drink to that. Where did the hooch go?

CAITLIN strokes her son's neck.

CAITLIN. Well done, darling, did you have fun?

OISIN (*semi-stern*). Get off me, would ya?

He gets up and gets a glass of water. CAITLIN *notices his coldness.*

Enter QUINN *drying his face on a towel, etc.*

They all cheer.

SHANE. There he is!

JJ (*simultaneous*). Boss man!

DIARMAID (*simultaneous*). The Mighty Quinn!

CAITLIN. So how did it go?

QUINN. It's all in except the low field. The ground's still too wet. The bailer's on the jip. And someone's left a chainsaw somewhere. Otherwise we're grand.

MICHAEL. We're in!

ALL. We're in!

CAITLIN. Well, that's something. That's that then.

QUINN. Aye, it is… Cheers.

ALL. Cheers!

MERCY, NUNU, HONOR *and* SHENA *enter from upstairs.*

DIARMAID (*simultaneous*). Here they come!

SHANE (*simultaneous*). Look out. Here comes trouble!

JJ (*simultaneous*). Will you look at that now!

MERCY. Evening, boys!

The CARNEYS *and the* CORCORANS *sing the third verse of 'Monto'.*

Enter MARY, *following the* GIRLS *down from upstairs.*

Everyone sings the refrain.

MARY *arrives downstairs.*

MARY. So am I to understand we may just scrape through another winter?

QUINN. With luck, aye.

DIARMAID (*simultaneous*). Get in there!

JJ (*simultaneous*). That's the way!

Cheers.

CAITLIN. Everyone, sit. It's going cold. Wait. Where's Aunt Pat?

UNCLE PAT. She'll be through for the pudding she said.

CAITLIN. Well, now…

They all sit. The food is served.

UNCLE PAT. Before we begin. A toast.

MICHAEL. A toast!

JJ. Silence!

ALL. Silence… Hush…!

UNCLE PAT. In 494 BC, Darius the Great stopped the Persian War to give the Greeks time to harvest their grapes. Because even a war-thirsty blood-monger like Darius knew, the harvest is sacred. The harvest is breath and life and spirit. And hope. Lord knows we need some of that right now.

Pause.

I shall close with the words of Henry Thoreau. 'The true Harvest of my Life is intangible. A little stardust caught. A portion of the rainbow I have clutched.'

Cheers. Whoops.

JJ (*simultaneous*). There now!

SHANE (*simultaneous*). Deadly!

MICHAEL (*simultaneous*). Nice one, big lad!

DIARMAID (*simultaneous*). Moving. Deeply moving.

UNCLE PAT. Without further ado, our host, Quinn Carney.

Cheers. QUINN *stands. Lots of table-banging. Cheering. Sssshh-ing.*

DIARMAID (*simultaneous*). Quinn, boy!!

MERCY / HONOR / SHENA (*chanting, simultaneous*). Dad! Dad! Dad! Dad! Dad!

MICHAEL (*simultaneous*). Quiet now.

JJ (*simultaneous*). Hark ye…

Pause.

QUINN. Once again we welcome the Corcoran mob to our table. Thanks for putting your shoulders to the wheel. No one got hurt, no one died. I can send you all home to your ma in one piece.

MICHAEL (*simultaneous, to* DECLAN). Just about, eh?

DIARMAID (*simultaneous, to* DECLAN). Ya wee berk!

Cheers.

QUINN. This was Big Jack's farm. And his father's father before him. Now it's my name on the letters the Department of Agriculture send to threaten us.

MICHAEL. Bastards!

JJ. Aye, Bastards!

Booing.

QUINN. One day it won't be my name. It won't be my land. It'll be James Joseph Carney's.

Cheering. Jeering.

James Joseph Carney. Stand up.

DIARMAID. Get up there, big man!

MICHAEL (*simultaneous*). On ya feet, boy!

SHANE (*simultaneous*). Jimbo!

MERCY / HONOR / NUNU (*simultaneous*). JJ! JJ! JJ!

SHENA (*simultaneous*). Don't scunder yerself now!

JJ stands.

JJ. Right enough.

QUINN. When these fifty acres are yours, and you're stood where I am, with your first harvest in, young and old at all sides, I want you to remember something. That a man who takes care of his family, is a man who can look himself in the eye in the morning. I hope you find as strong a rock as I have in Mary.

Silence. He stops.

To Mary…

ALL. To Mary. / To Ma…

QUINN. Finally, on behalf of this entire clan, I'd like to thank Caitlin for this wonderful food. And for everything she's done for this family over these past ten years.

ALL. To Caitlin. / Caitlin!

OISIN. To Caitlin.

Pause. They eat.

CAITLIN stands.

CAITLIN. Can I just say, thank you… to everyone in this household.

Pause.

When we came, we came with nothing. And the first morning, Quinn took Oisin out into the yard, he was four years old, and he took some wood and some nails and a hammer and Oisin watched as Quinn made him his own bed. I want to say thank you for that. (*Beat.*) And to my beautiful son, Oisin. I just want to say, Oisin, thank you for being so…

for being so wonderful to me… and making the wee ones a beautiful kite…

MICHAEL. Sure, Oisin banjaxed the kite.

JJ. Jeez… Have you forgotten that, Aunt Cait?

CAITLIN. No. No. I just want to say –

OISIN. Shut up, Mum. It's embarrassing.

CAITLIN. I just wanted to say –

OISIN. I said, shut up.

QUINN. Oisin –

CAITLIN. It's all right.

QUINN. No. Oisin. You don't speak to your mother like that. Not under this roof.

CAITLIN. Quinn. Please. Let him be. Everything's fine. Please. It's fine. Cheers, all. Here's to the harvest.

ALL. The harvest!

Silence.

MARY. An excellent speech, Quinn. Thank you. (*Beat.*) And Caitlin too.

Pause.

JJ. Will you not give us a song, Tom Kettle? An English song now.

TOM KETTLE. Me? Oh, I'm not much of a singer. But I do know a poem.

UNCLE PAT. See. Tom Kettle knows poetry. He's the full package. *L'omo universale*, so he is.

DIARMAID. Do you know a poem then, Tom Kettle? Sure, we'd love to hear it. Wouldn't we, boys?

TOM KETTLE. I found it at the library and I learned it. I sat there till it went dark. It is by… I can't remember. But it's very old.

DIARMAID. I'm genuinely looking forward to this.

MICHAEL. What's it called, Tom Kettle?

DIARMAID. Yeah, what's it called?

TOM KETTLE. It's called 'The Silent Lover', by Sir Walter
    Raleigh. It's about a silent lover.

SHANE. You don't say.

MICHAEL. Quiet, all.

JJ. Let's hear it.

Silence.

TOM KETTLE.
        Passions are likened best to floods and streams:
        The shallow murmur, but the deep are dumb;
        So, when affections yield discourse, it seems
        The bottom is but shallow whence they come.
        They that are rich in words –

Pause.

DIARMAID. Is that it?

Silence.

DECLAN. That can't be it. Surely.

Pause.

TOM KETTLE.
        Those that are rich in words, in words discover,
        That they are poor in that which makes a lover.
        Wrong not Sweet Empress of my heart.
        The merit of true passion,
        With thinking that he feels no smart,
        That sues for no compassion –
        Silence in love bewrays more woe
        Than words, though ne'er so witty:
        A beggar that is dumb, you know,
        May challenge double pity.
        Then wrong not, dearest to my heart,
        My true, though secret, passion:
        He smarteth most that hides his smart,
        And sues for no compassion.

They clap, cheer.

(*Relieved.*) It's extremely sad when you stop to think about it. How someone could love someone and them not know it. Passions are likened best to floods and streams, see…

DIARMAID. Jesus Christ. Is he going to do it again?

MICHAEL. Enough English woe. This is supposed to be a feast.

MICHAEL *is up. He has a tape in the tape deck. He turns it up.*

MARY. Michael, turn that off. We're eating.

MICHAEL. Now, Ma. You know as well as me, there's no eating at a Carney Feast.

DIARMAID (*simultaneous*). Here we go!

JJ (*simultaneous*). Crack on now!

SHENA (*simultaneous*). That's the way!

NUNU (*simultaneous*). I want to dance! I want to dance!

Huge whoops. The children are ecstatic. Everybody gets up. The table is pushed back.

An impromptu ceidlidh erupts.

Spirited. Anxious. Intense.

MICHAEL *takes* NUNU*'s hands.*

HONOR *spins with* UNCLE PAT.

QUINN *dances with* SHENA. *With* HONOR. *With* NUNU.

AUNT MAGGIE *watches everything.*

The song ends. Applause. Cheers. Between songs.

UNCLE PAT. Quinn. Why don't you dance with Caitlin there? She looks so lovely tonight.

Cheers. MARY *watches.*

CAITLIN. Aye, Quinn Carney. Why don't you dance with me?

Everyone eggs them on.

MARY. Dance with Cait, man. I'm exhausted.

QUINN *looks at her.*

JJ. Dance with your sister-in-law, man.

QUINN. Oh, you wanna dance, do you?

CAITLIN. Yes I do.

The KIDS *all clap and cheer.*

Over by the tape machine, SHANE *has swapped tapes.*

SHANE. You want to dance, Aunt Cait? Dance to this. (*To* ALL.) You country folk want to hear a tune?

He puts on 'Teenage Kicks' by The Undertones.

The CORCORAN BOYS *instantly all start pogoing and going crazy.*

The CARNEY BOYS *watch. Look at each other.*

MARY *puts her fingers in her ears.*

CAITLIN *starts dancing with the* BOYS. *Wildly. With drunken abandon.*

OISIN *watches.*

QUINN *watches, as* CAITLIN *starts dancing wildly with* SHANE.

Enter AUNT PAT. *She looks at the scene.*

AUNT PAT *slowly walks over to the counter. Pours herself a drink. Drains it.*

The music throbs. CAITLIN *dances with* SHANE.

Suddenly AUNT PAT *switches off the tape player.*

Complaints from the CORCORANS.

CAITLIN *steadies herself, as if waking up.*

MICHAEL. What are you pissing on the strawberries for, Aunt Pat? Put the boys' song back on.

Silence. AUNT PAT *turns. Silence.*

AUNT PAT. Michael Devine has starved himself to death.

Silence.

Michael Devine, Thomas McElwee, Kieran Doherty. Kevin Lynch. Martin Hurson, Joe McDonnell. Patsy O'Hara. Raymond McCreesh. Francies Hughes. Bobby Sands.

Silence.

QUINN. To the hunger strikers.

ALL. To the Hunger Strikers.

Silence. And out of it, SHANE *begins to sing.*

SHANE.
> I'll sing you a song of a row in the town,
> When the green flag went up and the Crown rag came
>   down,
> 'Twas the neatest and sweetest thing ever you saw,
> And they played that great game they call Erin go Bragh.

SHANE *and* DIARMAID.
> God bless gallant Pearse and our comrades who died
> Tom Clark, MacDonagh, MacDiarmada, McBryde,
> And here's to James Connolly who gave one hurrah,
> And faced the machine guns for Erin go Bragh.
> Into the Porch –

Enter MAGENNIS, MALONE, *and* MULDOON *into the boot room. The revellers can't see them yet.*

SHANE, DIARMAID *and* AUNT PAT.
> Now glory to old Dublin, and here's her renown,
> In the long generation her fame will go down,
> And our children will tell how their forefathers saw,
> The red blaze of freedom on Erin Go Braugh.

MULDOON *enters the kitchen.*

MAGENNIS *and* MALONE *wait in the porch.*

MULDOON. Good evening…

Pause.

MARY. Mr Muldoon. Come in. Come in.

MULDOON. Thank you, Mrs Carney.

MARY. Welcome. Your friends can come in.

MULDOON. If it's all the same they'll wait outside.

MARY. Well, if you're certain, can get wild cold out there at this time of year.

MULDOON. Is this your family, now?

MARY. Everybody, this is Mr Muldoon, an old friend from Derry. Mr Muldoon, this is our Uncle Pat.

UNCLE PAT. Good evening.

MARY. That's our Aunt Maggie there. And this is our Aunt Pat.

AUNT PAT. It's an honour, sir. Truly it is.

MULDOON. And who are these pretty wee things…

MARY. These are our girls, Nunu, Mercy, Honor and Shena. This is Michael. Our son. This is Jim Joe, our eldest.

They shake hands.

JJ. Hello.

MARY. And these are our nephews from Derry. The Corcorans.

MULDOON. Pleased to meet you.

DECLAN. And you, Mr Muldoon.

DIARMAID. Mr Muldoon. It's an honour.

MULDOON *stops. Points at* SHANE.

MULDOON. Don't I know you?

SHANE. Shane Corcoran.

MULDOON. That's right, Shane.

DIARMAID. I'm his brother Diarmaid. We're Molly Carney's boys.

MULDOON. I never forget a face. You over helping your uncle? Well, that's good of you. Sure, it's noble to lend a hand where it's needed. Tell me, son, what time is it?

SHANE. It's just gone a quarter past ten…

MULDOON. A quarter past ten. Thank you.

Pause.

SHENA. This is Tom Kettle. Our friend.

MARY. He helps here on the farm.

MULDOON. It's a pleasure.

TOM KETTLE. Sorry I didn't catch your name.

MULDOON. It's Muldoon.

TOM KETTLE. Would you like an apple, Mr Muldoon. I grew it in my garden. It's a Royal Gala.

MULDOON. Sure, that doesn't sound like an Armagh apple.

TOM KETTLE. I sent off for the seeds. In 1953, to celebrate the Queen's Coronation. I grew it from seed and now it's over twelve feet high. Would you like one?

MULDOON. What's an Englishman doing all the way out here now?

AUNT PAT. That is a good question.

MARY. Tom Kettle's been here since he was a boy.

Pause.

MULDOON. Thank you. I'm not hungry.

TOM KETTLE. Hold on. What's this?

He pulls out a rabbit. Holds it out for MULDOON. MULDOON *doesn't take it. Pause.*

MARY. Tom, put that away now.

TOM KETTLE (*still holding out the rabbit*). I'm sorry, Mrs Carney. I can see now this is not the time.

MARY. It's all right.

TOM KETTLE. It's just it was quite loud in here. I don't like it when it's loud and now I'm sweating buckets.

MARY. It's all right, Tom. Put the rabbit away.

TOM KETTLE. Absolutely.

He does, retreating.

Pause.

MARY. And this is Caitlin Carney.

MULDOON. Sure, I remember Caitlin.

MARY. And this is my husband, Quinn, who you know.

MULDOON. Well, now. Quinn. It's been a while, so it has.

QUINN. Jimmy.

Pause.

MULDOON. So is the harvest in?

QUINN. Aye, it is.

MULDOON. Is it wheat you're growing?

QUINN. Barley. Wheat. Some oats.

MULDOON. And where does that end up?

QUINN. They ship it.

MULDOON. Where to?

QUINN. Poland.

MULDOON. Poland?

AUNT PAT. The 1976 Agricultural Act decreed weather in South Armagh too damp to grow crop for human consumption. Since when Quinn's wheat gets packed up and shipped off to Poland for animal feed.

MULDOON. And what type of animals would they be?

AUNT PAT. Pigs.

MULDOON. Pigs, eh? Polish pigs?

Pause.

UNCLE PAT. So tell me, Mr Muldoon. What brings you all the way out here at this time of night? Sure, it must be important now?

MULDOON. Well, firstly, I've come to bring condolences.

UNCLE PAT. Condolences? For what?

Pause.

MULDOON. Is it not common knowledge? You must forgive me.

CAITLIN. Oisin. I need to speak to you, please.

MARY. Is everything all right?

UNCLE PAT. Has something happened?

CAITLIN. Oisin, let's go outside.

AUNT PAT. What's happened?

MICHAEL. What's happened, Da?

OISIN. I know what's happened. They found my da. In a bog down by the border. He's got a bullet in his head. He's dead. He's been dead for years.

Silence.

MARY. Quinn. Is this true?

QUINN. All the young ones in bed now. Everybody.

OISIN *runs out of the house. The others begin to exit.*

JJ. Aunt Cait.

MICHAEL. I'm so sorry, Auntie Cait.

CAITLIN. It's all right.

UNCLE PAT. Caitlin. I'm so sorry. Truly I am.

CAITLIN. It's all right, Pat. Everything's fine.

CAITLIN *exits, following* OISIN. MARY *goes to* QUINN.

QUINN. It's okay. Mary.

MARY *goes upstairs.*

UNCLE PAT. Quinn?

QUINN. It's fine, Pat.

UNCLE PAT. Well, then. I'll check on the weans. Goodnight.

QUINN. It's bedtime, Shane.

SHANE. You know, Uncle Quinn, I think I'll take a wee stroll before turning in. A nice moonlit stroll down by the river there. Maybe a swim? What do you say, Uncle Quinn?

Beat.

QUINN. Be back here in an hour.

SHANE *smiles*.

SHANE. Thank you, Uncle Quinn. Goodnight.

Exit SHANE *and his brothers*.

AUNT PAT. Mr Muldoon. I had a brother. He was at the GPO there in '16 and he gave his life that day. He would want me to shake the hand of the man who fought the Battle of the Bogside. Stood up to Internment. You are the spirit, sir, the brave true spirit.

QUINN. You leave us alone now, Pat.

Exit AUNT PAT.

QUINN *and* MULDOON *are left alone*.

MALONE *and* MAGENNIS *wait outside in the porch*.

MULDOON. I'm sorry, Quinn. I had no idea that the information about Seamus had not reached the family. The disappearance of a loved one is a harrowing event. I cannot fathom how the years of uncertainty –

QUINN. Who came up with the idea? (*Beat.*) Don't get me wrong, it's brilliant. Sure, a kneecapping hurts. Even with a death. There's a body. She can grieve. In time the pain finds a home. But take a man out to a bog in the middle of nowhere. Put a bullet in his head. Then send friends to the widow to tell her they've seen him. On a ferry to Liverpool. The horses in Wicklow. Give that woman hope. Keep the wound open. It's genius, sure it is. A fantastic use of resources.

Beat.

MULDOON....I cannot fathom how the years of uncertainty must have taken their toll on you, on Caitlin, and on her boy.

That's why I wanted to come here personally to assure you
that, whatever happened to Seamus all those years ago,
whatever went on, that the IRA had absolutely nothing to do
with it. I know that there have been rumours, allegations –

QUINN (*interrupting*). I'll tell you what went on. My brother
was jammed in a van. Whisked off to some barn, some
cottage. Interrogated. Beaten. His confession was taped.
He was driven out to some bog, his hands were tied and
while he pleaded for his life and begged Jesus for mercy he
was shot in the back of the head. Within a week the rumours
start. Seamus was an informer. Seamus is dead. Seamus is
alive. Seamus is on the run. His family is ostracised. By
Christmas his mother's dead from the stress. His widow is
insane with fear. His boy has no father. (*Beat.*) *Was that fun,
Jimmy?* Walking in here, in the middle of it all. Looking
Caitlin in the eye. Seeing Oisin? Was that a thrill now?

MULDOON. Be careful, Quinn –

QUINN. One month before Seamus disappeared, I came to you
and I told you I wanted out. I told you why. I said I had
enough blood on my hands. You listened. You said you
understood. Four weeks later, to the day, Seamus disappeared.
(*Beat.*) Condolences, Jimmy. Fucking *condolences*?

Pause.

Why are you really here? What do you want?

Pause.

MULDOON. This is a critical time, Quinn. The hunger strikes
have garnered an unprecedented global focus. We stand a
chance of becoming a real political force. That's why it's
crucial, moving forward, that when the news concerning
Seamus is released, that no wrongful allegations be made
which might damage our efforts, or jeopardise our goals.

Pause. QUINN *studies him.*

QUINN. Do you remember back in the cage there, when the
screws found a Parker Pen? It was my pen. You said it was
your pen. They took you down into the basement and they
jumped up and down on your feet. They put you up against

a boiling radiator and roasted the skin off your back. And you
kept saying that it was your pen. Do you remember that day?

Pause.

MULDOON. Sure, I don't remember that. You'd think I would
now.

QUINN. You don't remember.

MULDOON. Are you sure it wasn't my pen? Sure, mine was
probably bangled halfway up my hole. Along with a lighter.
Baccy. Up there in the old larder. The suitcase there.
(*Chuckles.*)

QUINN. You have a burn across your back. A scar about twelve
inches long. Clean across your spine.

MULDOON. Strange. But now I think of it, it sounds highly
improbable. Can you imagine taking a hammering like that
for someone and not recall it? (*Beat.*) Well, I'll have to
double-check that when I get home. I'll ask Susan to have a
wee look. Who knows. You might be right. You might have
something there.

QUINN. That man you took that beating for, suffered for, for
a fucking pen. That man *walked away*. That's hard to bear
now. A man might want revenge for something like that.
He might *still* want revenge.

MULDOON. Sure, there'll be no talk of revenge, Quinn. And if
you'll excuse me, I think you're overestimating yourself.
You're not a soldier any more. You're a farmer. A busy one
too. So what I merely ask is this. That you accept that
Seamus's disappearance was a tragedy which had absolutely
nothing to do with us. And in doing so, that you provide me
with assurances. That if a reporter were to telephone. That
there'll be no hot-headedness. That you and everyone under
this roof will be trusted to behave responsibly. If you can
provide me with that assurance, then you have my word –

QUINN. No. The answer is no. I'm gonna drink this drink, and
bury my brother. And I will ask you to leave my house… and
leave this family be.

Pause.

MULDOON. I remember when you heard your first child was born. You showed me a photograph of him, when he was only a few weeks old. You looked me in the eye and said you'd watch that baby burn in a fire, if it meant a free Ireland. And I thought, 'That is what it takes. *That* is the cost of freedom. The price is unimaginable. And here is a man who knows that. And is willing to pay it.' How many harvests have you brought in since then, Quinn? That's a lot of sun on your back. All those smiling wee faces.

QUINN. Get out of my house.

MULDOON *moves to the door. Stops.*

MULDOON. By the way. How's Mary? I hear she's been unwell. It must be difficult for her all these years, sharing a home with another woman. I don't suppose that was ever her plan. It shows a big heart. Good for the boy too. But it must make it all a bit topsy-turvy. A bit lopsided sometimes. She's an attractive woman, Caitlin. Any man can see that. No less attractive than she was ten years ago. More so, if anything. In any case, I'm just saying, it must be difficult. A difficult arrangement. Hello, young man.

QUINN *turns. Enter* OISIN, *from the shadows.*

I want you to know how sorry I am for your loss. As I was explaining to your uncle, I appreciate the toll that years of uncertainty can extract. It's a terrible thing that has happened. A terrible, terrible thing.

He offers his hand. OISIN *shakes it.*

Enter CAITLIN.

CAITLIN. Oisin. Come here, please.

QUINN. Cait –

CAITLIN. Come here, please, Oisin. Now.

OISIN. Ma –

CAITLIN. Come here, Oisin. (*Takes hold of him.*)

OISIN. Let go of me.

He shrugs her off.

I heard you talking this morning. You knew Dad was dead and you never told me.

CAITLIN. Oisin –

OISIN. Fuck off. You're a liar. You're both of youse liars.

He runs out.

QUINN. Let him go.

MULDOON. Caitlin, I was just saying to your son how sorry I am for your loss. At least now you know the worst of it. But I'm not going to pretend it isn't a horrible event, even after all this time.

CAITLIN. I'm glad you came here today, Mr Muldoon. Because it gives me the chance to say something I've wanted to say for a long time.

Pause.

MULDOON. And what would that be?

CAITLIN. Six months before Seamus disappeared he bought himself his first car. A Morris Marina 1.8 Super Deluxe Coupé. Sienna orange. Second hand. Five years old. A hundred pounds down. Spoiler on the back, and up there on the windshield, 'Caitlin and Elvis'. Every night, back from the plant, he's out there with the soap and the chamois, getting that thing like a mirror. We called her 'The Other Woman'. 'Sure, you take more care over that car…'

Pause.

About a week after he disappeared, I was here, at this house, and a man called by. It was a friend of Seamus, a friend from school, saying Seamus'd been spotted at Belfast terminal, getting on the ferry. We went down to the docks together, and in a street nearby, there was the car parked in the street there. The Marina. I took one look at that car and I knew instantly that Seamus was dead.

Pause.

You see, Mr Muldoon, it was parked under this tree. Under this huge sycamore. There's no way on God's earth he would park that car under a big tree like that, and let the pigeons, the gulls, the gannets, the shitehawks crap all over it...

Pause.

Sure, we'd drive a round for half an hour to find a spot where there was no trees. It would drive me crazy.

Pause.

If you know a man. If you really know him...

Pause.

It didn't work, see. I knew. You never got me, Mr Muldoon. You never got me.

Enter MARY, *holding the baby.*

MARY. Is everything all right in here?

MULDOON. Everything is fine, Mary.

QUINN. Mr Muldoon is leaving.

MARY. Will you not stay for a bite to eat, Mr Muldoon?

MULDOON. Quinn's right. I think I've interfered quite enough with your evening.

He goes to the door.

I'm going to leave now, Mary. But I'll return in the morning, when you've had more of a chance to absorb the terrible news, and Quinn has had the opportunity to digest our conversation, and my request. (*Re: the baby.*) Is that your latest addition there, Mary. What's his name?

MARY. His name is Bobby.

MULDOON. Bobby. That's a nice name. You have a beautiful family, Mary. A beautiful family.

MARY. Thank you, Mr Muldoon.

MULDOON. Goodnight to you. Goodnight, Quinn.

Exit MULDOON, MAGENNIS *and* MALONE.

MARY. Would you like a cup of tea now, Caitlin?

CAITLIN. No, thank you. Mary.

MARY. Mr Muldoon said he has a request.

QUINN. It's nothing.

MARY. How can it be nothing now?

QUINN. He wants to make a contribution to the cost of the funeral…

Beat.

MARY. Well, that's extremely generous of him.

QUINN. I need to speak to Caitlin.

MARY. Well, can't it wait? It's extremely late. And I'm sure Caitlin needs this time.

QUINN. Of course.

MARY. You should come to bed now, Quinn. It's been a long day.

QUINN. We'll speak in the morning.

MARY. You make yourself a nice cup there, Caitlin. Don't worry about us. Goodnight, Caitlin.

CAITLIN. Goodnight, Mary.

Exit QUINN *and* MARY *upstairs.*

CAITLIN *is alone.*

She breaks down.

Enter TOM KETTLE.

TOM KETTLE. Good evening, Caitlin.

CAITLIN. Good evening, Tom Kettle.

TOM KETTLE. I came to say sorry. About Seamus and all.

CAITLIN. What? Right. Thank you. Thank you, Tom Kettle.

TOM KETTLE. It's not right, a wife should wait ten years to find she's not. And those were long years. And your boy. He's a good lad. Point him at something and he's right there. Just last week him and me put the window back in the

lean-to. It had swung open, in the wind. The latch had split
clean off. He did it all. With the hammer. Nails. And the
putty. I'm stood by. Him with the hammer, and the putty.
I bet he never told you neither.

CAITLIN. He never did.

TOM KETTLE. And he told me, he said the bad dreams have
stopped. That's good, now.

CAITLIN. It is.

TOM KETTLE. And so I picked you some flowers, to cheer
you up a bit. There's poppies and forget-me-nots. They're
from my garden.

CAITLIN. Ah, Tom Kettle.

TOM KETTLE. Have they cheered you up?

CAITLIN. I dare say they have a little. Thank you.

TOM KETTLE. You're a good woman, Cait Carney. And a good
woman. A good woman shouldn't be alone. A good woman
needs a man.

Pause.

CAITLIN. Tom –

TOM KETTLE. Now before you say anything, I need you to
hear me out, all in one go. Because I've thought it through,
see, and if I don't say it all in one go I'll get lost. (*Beat.*)
There's them about would say I'm not the full bucket. But
I know north from south. I ain't never fallen off nothing, nor
burned nothing down. I can whittle and carry logs all day.
I only smoke at Christmas time and that's one Hamlet. I can
cook too. (*Beat.*) It's many a night I've thought of you. But
I knew it wasn't right with Seamus missing and all. But now
those days have gone. They're in the past and everyone can
move on. And there was that time we were in the paddock,
throwing snowballs, and you hit me with one right here. And
I fell down like I was dead, and you came over, everyone
was there, but still you came right over and kneeled down
and you kissed me here. Like to make it better. And you give
me a smile I can see now. I don't have to close my eyes to

see it. I can see it here. The long and the short is, ever since that day I loved you, Cait. Through the springs and the summers. But I done my best and kept it quiet. Pick a card.

Pause.

CAITLIN. Tom.

TOM KETTLE. Pick one. Any one. Come on. Don't be shy.

She comes forward. Picks a card.

Don't show me it. Have you remembered it?

She nods.

Puts it back in the pack.

CAITLIN. Tom –

TOM KETTLE. Hang on. Almost there…

He throws the pack in the air, the cards flutter down.

Is this yours? Is this yours, Cait?

Between his forefinger and thumb, something shiny.

A ring.

He gets down on one knee.

I will love you until your final breath, and a thousand years beyond. And now all I ask is, give me your answer do. Give me your answer, do.

Enter SHANE.

SHANE. Excuse me.

CAITLIN. It's all right, Shane.

SHANE. I hope I'm not interrupting anything here.

CAITLIN. You're not interrupting.

SHANE. I'll just walk once around the barn there. Evening, Aunt Cait. Evening, Tom Kettle.

Exit SHANE.

TOM KETTLE. Damn it. Dagnabbit. I planned this. I really did. I wrote it all down about twenty times. And I have to say, this hasn't gone as I planned it.

CAITLIN. You're a good man, Tom Kettle. A good, good man. I can't marry you.

TOM KETTLE. I understand.

CAITLIN. It's not the time.

TOM KETTLE. I understand.

CAITLIN. You're family, Tom. You always were.

TOM KETTLE. I understand.

CAITLIN. Oh, Tom.

She hugs him. He tries to kiss her.

No, Tom. No.

TOM KETTLE. I understand. I understand.

CAITLIN. You must go now.

TOM KETTLE. I understand. Well, I'm going to be off now. There's all sorts to do in the morning.

He goes to leave. Stops.

Anyway, my point is, you want to get those poppies in water. They don't last long picked… Goodnight, all.

He leaves.

CAITLIN *is alone.*

Silence.

AUNT MAGGIE (*sings*).
　　My young love said to me 'My mother won't mind
　　And my father won't slight you for your lack of kind'
　　And she laid her hand on me and this she did say
　　'Oh, it will not be long, love, till our wedding-day.'

Pause.

Francis Maloney, you're late again, you rogue. Sure, what's keeping you now? Out there flashing your mane to all the ladies. Sure, I was a fool to marry such a handsome man. If I've learned one thing in this life, it's that Love is nothing but Sorrow. You'll be the death of me, Francis Maloney. When are you going to come home? When, Francis? When?

AUNT MAGGIE *turns to* CAITLIN, *and holds her gaze*.

Blackout.

End of Act Two.

ACT THREE

The dead of night. The Carneys' kitchen.

The CARNEY BOYS *and the* CORCORAN BOYS. *All drinking whiskey. Smoking roll-ups.* JJ *is draped in the Irish flag.* JJ *and* MICHAEL *are wearing Celtic shirts.*

DIARMAID. We got the first bus from Waterside and it's coming down stair rods all the way. 6 a.m. and the coach is sardines, we're stood up all the way, riding into Belfast on the way to the funeral. The driver's got the radio on full-blast and your man there's sayin' eighty, ninety thousand folk are lining the street. The bus is red-hot, steamed up, dripping down the windows. Banners, flags, all furled, but we haven't got no flag nor banner, all we've got is a fuckin' Bic. This Bic biro. Right? So I take it and write your man's name on my hand. And Shane writes it on his. 'Bobby Sands. RIP.' And we write it on the back of our jackets. But the fucking biro packs in. The nib breaks. All it says on my back is 'BO'.

JJ. Class.

DIARMAID. I'm gonna walk around all day with 'BO' on my back.

MICHAEL. Fuckin' priceless.

DIARMAID. Like it's some warning. Some sign for the rest of the mourners to steer fucking clear.

MICHAEL. Love it.

DIARMAID. Then this old girl there, eighty years old, stood the whole fucking way, she reaches in her bag and she fishes out a can. A fuckin' aerosol. 'Turn round, wean.' And we stand side by side, backs to her and she sprays 'Justice' across both our backs in black fucking aerosol.

JJ. Crack on, Grandma!

DIARMAID. The whole of the bus puts up this cheer. And they start chanting. 'Justice, justice, justice.'

Pause.

And we ride into Belfast, with the whole bus chanting, singing, all the way into the city. (*Swigs again.*) By the time we got to St Luke's and the whole place is jammed to standing. They've rigged up speakers but there's four or five helicopters circling the chapel. You can't see or hear a fuckin' thing, just the backs of steaming coats and helicopters.

DECLAN. Choppers.

DIARMAID. What?

DECLAN. Choppers. Call 'em choppers.

DIARMAID. Who's tellin' this story. You or me?

DECLAN. I'm just saying.

DIARMAID. Sure, you weren't even there. It was just me and Shane.

DECLAN. I'm just saying you could say choppers. Choppers would make the story more, you know... cooler. More exciting.

DIARMAID. Is that a fact, Kojak? Fuckin' Six Million Dollar Man over here.

DECLAN. Get to fuck.

JJ. Go on with the story.

DIARMAID. So they bring the coffin out, and that's the first glimpse of the boy from Twinbrook. Six-deep, for nine miles. We crawl our way to the front. And you can see it coming. This black car. With Bobby in the back, draped in the tricolore. And it passes. And as it does, the whole crowd starts chanting your man's name. 'Bobby Sands! Bobby Sands!' The hearse stops outside the gates of the cemetery. And they lift your man out, lift out the coffin and place it on tressels. There's wreaths, Hail Marys, Joyful Mysteries. A piper playing the 'Long Kesh' anthem. Then from the crowd come these four RA, in masks and berets, and draw their pistols and – (*Makes a gunshot sound three times*.) over the coffin. At the graveside, they've got a bullhorn, and you can hear 'em clean over the helicopters. And he quoted Bobby… They used Bobby's own words.

MICHAEL. What did he say?

DIARMAID. 'They have nothing in their whole imperial arsenal… They have nothing in their whole'… ah, how the fuck does it go?

DECLAN. You've blown it now. You told the whole story and you fucked up the end.

DIARMAID. You weren't even there.

DECLAN. You're at this big historic event. And you blow the punchline. What if the Apostles were at your man Jesus's crucifixion there and they forgot the key bit. 'Lord, Lord, why have you for–… Why have you…'

They all laugh.

SHANE. 'They have nothing in their whole imperial arsenal that can break the spirit of one Irishman who doesn't want to be broken. I am hungry only for justice.'

Pause.

MICHAEL. Well, now. That's a hell of a thing to say. That's a hell of a turn of phrase.

Pause.

JJ. Shane, boy. Earlier, when Mr Muldoon got here, he's saying his hellos and he stops by you like he knows ye.

SHANE. He does know me.

JJ. How does he know you?

DIARMAID. Are you going to tell them?

JJ. Fuckin' tell us, man.

MICHAEL. Aye, tell us. How do you know Muldoon?

SHANE. Nah, you're all right.

MICHAEL. Ah, come on, Shane.

SHANE. Nah, I'm not telling.

DIARMAID. Fucking tell 'em.

SHANE. All right, I'll tell yas. Just to shut you up an' all. But first you have to all take a nip.

MICHAEL. Right you are.

JJ. Fair dos.

They pass the bottle. Everyone has a swig.

SHANE. How's that?

JJ (*coughing*). Regal.

MICHAEL. Come on, man.

Pause.

SHANE. Three, four weeks after the funeral, I'm back in town and I'm doing my paper round, going door to door, on the front page there's the news. McCreesh and O'Hara have both starved to death on the same morning. The third and fourth to perish. So I'm delivering the papers when your wee fella rides up on his Grifter there, spotty little cunt about nine years old, and he stops and he asks me if I'm Shane Cocoran. I tell him to do one. But, 'Are you Shane Corcoran? Pat Corcoran's boy?' 'Who wants to know?' 'Mr Muldoon.'

MICHAEL. Get to fuck.

DIARMAID. Your very man.

JJ. What did he want?

MICHAEL. Fuckin' Muldoon?

DIARMAID. Listen now.

SHANE. He says Mr Muldoon wants to talk to you.

MICHAEL. Are you shitting yourself? I'd be shitting myself.

JJ. I'm shitting myself sat here hearing about it.

SHANE. So your wee man on the Grifter says go down McCartney's Café, nine o'clock Saturday morning. And he burns off. So Saturday comes, I go down McCartney's, and I sit down, cup of tea, eyes on the clock. Nine sharp, your man walks in.

MICHAEL. Fuck me.

JJ. Fuck me.

MICHAEL. Muldoon? To meet you? Why?

SHANE. He sits down opposite and he looks at me and he says, 'Are you Shane Corcoran?' And I said yes. (*Beat*.) He starts asking me questions.

MICHAEL. What questions?

SHANE. About the paper round. What days. Which streets. He says there's a laundry van, Malone's Laundry. All he wants me to do is make a mental note of when I see it. Make a note of the time and where it stops. I say I haven't got a watch. And he looks at me and he says, 'I saw you there at the funeral last week. Over there in Milltown. Among the crowd.'

MICHAEL. He saw you. Muldoon saw you.

SHANE. 'I saw you there. At Bobby's funeral.' 'Yes, Mr Muldoon.' 'You boys had something written on your backs there. What was that now?'

Pause.

'Justice.'

Pause.

'And do you want justice, Shane?'

Pause.

'Yes, Mr Muldoon. I want justice. For Bobby. For Patsy. For us all.' And he goes to his wrist here, and he takes off his watch and he hands it to me. He says, 'Now you've got a watch.'

JJ. Bollocks.

DIARMAID. Show 'em.

He rolls up his sleeve.

JJ. That's his watch? That's Muldoon's watch?

DIARMAID. Check that out.

JJ. Fuck me.

DIARMAID. He walks in here. 'What's the fuckin' time?'

JJ. Fuck me.

DIARMAID. 'What's the fuckin' time. Eh? What's the fucking time?'

MICHAEL. That's a nice watch.

DIARMAID. Are you fuckin' kidding me? It's a fucking slimline digital. It's got a light. And a stopwatch. And it goes down to fifty metres.

DECLAN. Which'll be handy when Muldoon gives you the concrete shoes and shoves you in the Foyle. You'll be down there, you can switch on the little light and say, 'It's thirty-one minutes and nineteen seconds past eleven. And to think I'd be down here with absolutely no idea what time it was if it wasn't for that generous Mr Muldoon.'

JJ. So what happened next?

SHANE. So for the next few weeks I'm doing my round, and I see the laundry van there. Malone's Laundry. And I note the time, and where it goes. And each Friday your keed on his Grifter comes by, and I tell him. I don't write nothing down. I just remember. Four weeks ago I'm doing my rounds and I see it there on the front page. Malone's Laundry van blown sky-fucking-high in the Bishops Road. (*Beat.*) They put a parcel under it. Behind the courthouse there. Twenty pounds of Semtex. Guess what? They weren't laundrymen. It's a fucking meat wagon. RUC Black Ops. Every time they went past there's three of them crouched down in the back there taking pictures of the comings and goings.

DIARMAID. Not any more.

SHANE. Not any more. Now all three are in bits all over the Bishops Road. In nine bin bags.

DIARMAID. Splashed up the back of the courthouse there. Fucking dog food.

JJ. Fuck me.

DECLAN. Jeez, the way he tells it you'd think he planted the fuckin' thing himself.

DIARMAID. Get to fuck, Declan. It happened.

DECLAN. The RA had eight, nine keeds casing that van. Fergus Neal. Nookie Flynn. They're all of them's round town right now, bragging how Muldoon asked him to keep an eye out.

SHANE. Is that so, Declan? Am I just another wee fucker? Tell me, are they all wearing Mr Muldoon's fuckin' digital watch tonight?

DIARMAID. Tell 'em about the Palace Road thing.

SHANE. Nah, you're all right.

DIARMAID. Tell 'em.

SHANE. Nah. Bollocks to it. I'm done telling stories.

JJ. What happened in Palace Road?

MICHAEL. What happened?

SHANE. Nah, you're all right.

JJ. Ah… fucking hell. Come on.

DIARMAID. Tell 'em, Shane.

MICHAEL. What happened, Shane. What did you do?

Silence.

SHANE. Okay, but you're all gonna have to have another drink.

DIARMAID. And trust me, this one you're gonna need.

They drink.

JJ. Easy there, Declan.

MICHAEL. How's that now.

DECLAN. My legs feel wicked.

DIARMAID. Well, come on, man… Tell the story.

Pause.

SHANE. About a week after the bombing, I'm walking down the lane there and a car pulls up and it's Mr Muldoon. He asks me to get inside. We drive across town to this boarded-up house on the Palace Road.

Pause.

There's this clown they hauled in. This header from Springtown.

Pause.

They've got him tied to a chair there. Muldoon asked me to watch the door.

Pause.

JJ. What was it? A beating?

MICHAEL. Who was he?

SHANE. Search me.

JJ. Was he an Orangie?

SHANE. He was one of their own.

JJ. What did they do to him?

SHANE. This and that.

JJ. What did they do?

MICHAEL. What did they do, Shane?

DIARMAID. Can I say, Shane?

SHANE. Look at this bloodthirsty wee bastard.

JJ. Did he say anything?

SHANE. He was gagged.

JJ. Did they kill him?

MICHAEL. He was one of their own?

SHANE. He was a clown.

MICHAEL. He was RA though.

SHANE. All I know is he was Roman Catholic.

MICHAEL. Wait. How do you know? If he was gagged.

SHANE. Because he had this on.

He holds up a silver crucifix, on a chain around his neck.

JJ. Fucking hell, man.

DIARMAID. Check that out. Silver. The chain and all...

He dangles it there. They all come over and look at it.

JJ. Is that his?

SHANE. Not any more.

JJ. Fuckin' hell.

DIARMAID. What about that then? Eh? What about that?

DECLAN. A watch. A chain. You're getting yourself a nice little store of mementos there, Shane. You're having a good war, so you are.

JJ. So they were just beating on a Catholic boy?

DIARMAID. They was punishing him.

JJ. What for?

SHANE. Because he fucked up.

MICHAEL. Like Uncle Seamus.

DIARMAID. Come off it, man. That was all a long time ago.

MICHAEL. Was it, Shane? Because they found his body last Tuesday.

DIARMAID. Ah, come off it, Michael. Let's not be spoiling the evening and all.

MICHAEL. Uncle Seamus wore a cross just like that one.

DIARMAID. All right, boys –

MICHAEL. It was just the same.

SHANE. Look. I never knew the man. And sure, he was good craic. But I guarantee you one thing. If Seamus wakes up dead in a border bog with a bullet in the brain, then somehow, somewhere, some time, Seamus fucked up.

MICHAEL. That's your uncle.

DIARMAID. Will you twos knock it off now. You're wrecking my buzz, so you are.

MICHAEL. How do you know what Uncle Seamus did? You were six years old when he disappeared. Sure, I was five. Declan there was in his fuckin' nappy. None of us know what Uncle Seamus did.

Enter CAITLIN, *from outside*.

JJ. Someone's coming.

They hide their cigarettes. She enters.

CAITLIN. Have any of you boys seen Oisin?

MICHAEL. Oisin. No, Aunt Cait.

JJ. I haven't seen him.

DIARMAID. Me neither.

MICHAEL. Is he not in his bunk?

CAITLIN. Did you see him come through?

JJ. No one's come through, Aunt Cait.

MICHAEL. He could be in his bunk. Or out in the barn on the pallias there. Do you need a hand?

CAITLIN. No. I'm grand.

She exits. Silence.

MICHAEL. Jesus Christ.

JJ. Poor woman.

Pause.

DIARMAID. Sure, the birds were going crazy today. They're dive-bombing the combine, so they were.

JJ. It's swallows. They're feasting on the insects dislodged by the blades.

DIARMAID. It feels like a long year since the last harvest. A lot's happened.

JJ. It has an' all.

Pause.

DIARMAID. Here. What about the dancing, eh? Dancing like that. I've never seen her like that before.

JJ. She's in shock.

DIARMAID. I'm just saying, dancing like that…

SHANE. She had her hand on my arse at one point.

DIARMAID. I saw that.

JJ. Will you shut the fuck up now, Shane.

DECLAN. She's coming back.

Re-enter CAITLIN.

JJ. Is he not there, Aunt Cait?

CAITLIN. His bunk's not slept in. I've looked for him everywhere.

MICHAEL. Have you tried the far barn?

CAITLIN. I've looked in all the barns.

DIARMAID. Sure, he'll turn up, Aunt Cait. He's like a cat, that one. Slips in and out.

JJ. Do you want a hand? We can get the torches and have a wee search party.

CAITLIN. No. You boys make the harvest. Sure, you haven't seen one another in a year.

SHANE. Evening there, Aunt Cait. Would you like a wee drink?

CAITLIN. What? No.

SHANE. Are you sure now? We could put some music on?

JJ. Leave it, Shane.

MICHAEL. Sure, he's got a thousand hiding places. Have you looked in the wood?

JJ. Mike's right. He'll be up in the wood.

CAITLIN. I've checked.

MICHAEL. Did you check the German trenches?

JJ. Not in the trenches. He's got himself a little tree hide there, down by the brook.

MICHAEL. By the steps.

JJ. Along from the steps. By those old oil drums there. If you want I'll show youse.

CAITLIN. No, I know the spot.

SHANE. Are you sure you don't want a hand? Sure, I don't mind coming along. Keep you company and all...

CAITLIN. Don't drink too much of that whiskey now, Shane. And Michael. You all be in bed when I get back.

DIARMAID. Night, Aunt Cait.

DECLAN / JJ / MICHAEL. Night, Aunt Cait.

Exit CAITLIN.

Now we see that OISIN *has been listening.*

MICHAEL. Ten years. What does that do to a woman?

SHANE. Ah... She's a strong girl, that one. And a fine dancer.

JJ. Knock it off.

SHANE. I'm just saying she's got spirit. And it can't be easy being alone and all. That's if she is.

MICHAEL. What do you mean? Sure, Caitlin doesn't have anyone. Not all this time.

JJ. Not in ten years. How could she, man?

SHANE. Well, if Seamus had done what he was told she wouldn't be alone. His boy would have a father now. Not one getting dug up this week after ten years in the sod.

JJ. Fuckin' hell, Shane, will you leave it?

SHANE. I'm just saying. In war you need discipline. Not fucking clowns can't keep their mouths shut. Discipline. Courage. Loyalty.

MICHAEL. Are you in a war, Shane?

SHANE. Are you not, Michael?

DIARMAID. Let's change the subject.

JJ. Aye, change the subject.

Pause.

DECLAN. How do you know the Elephant Man is a Protestant?

DIARMAID. How?

DECLAN. Because he fucking looks like one.

They all laugh. Pause.

MICHAEL. And what would you be meaning by loyalty there?

SHANE. Sure, I don't want pick a fight with ya, Michael.

MICHAEL. Then just tell me. What did you mean by loyalty?

SHANE. I didn't mean nothing by it. Your father was a brave man. Respected. Sure, there's still men in town too scared to speak his name.

MICHAEL. And who told you all this? Because, as I recall, in 1971, you and me were six years old.

SHANE. My da.

MICHAEL. Your da's a drunk.

JJ. Michael…

DIARMAID. Whoa there…

SHANE. Is that so, Michael –

MICHAEL. You don't know who Quinn Carney was.

DECLAN. Will the both of youse calm down?

SHANE. All I'm saying is, at the end of the day, there's those willing to make sacrifices for their country and those that aren't. Quinn Carney is a good man. A family man. (*Beat.*) Sure, he likes to keep it in the family.

JJ. You shut your fucking mouth, Shane Corcoran.

DIARMAID. Stow it now, the both of youse.

SHANE. Have you any idea what it's like in town at the moment? The Brits are lifting whole areas. Streaking in, the Black Saracens. Busting the streetlights. Shooting dogs. Stripping Gran down to her girdle in the street. In The Bricklayers. Everyone up against the wall, the fuckin' Paras going along the top shelf, cartons of cigs in the old flak jacket. Liftings. Beatings. Proper fucking diggings. Houses raided three times a night. Petrol bombs. Nail bombs. Me and Diarmaid in the Shanty, we're in the alley there, the Paras've got the nine-mill Browning in my ear. 'I'm gonna scone you, you Irish fuck. Knock your fuckin' cunt in.' One of 'em sees I got the *Republican News* there sticking out my arse pocket. They've rolled it up and tried to shove it up my hole. Me and Finn Bailey, spread-eagled round the back of the bingo, this Para pulls the bolt of his Sterling down. 'Can you do an Irish jig?' I'll do no fucking Irish jig. I don't even know one. They kicked us in the bollocks so hard Finn had an epileptic fit. His ma went to the police station. Waited seven hours. They made her fill out a form. 'When did your boys get lifted and what happened?' Then they whip out the lighter there and burn the fucking form and drop it in her lap.

Pause.

A stop to all that. The land returned. That's what I mean by justice. Do you not want justice, Michael?

DIARMAID. Ah, come on now –

SHANE. Do you or do you not want justice?

MICHAEL. I'll tell you what I don't want. I don't want to watch the door while a Catholic boy gets hammered. I don't want to wear that boy's cross round my neck, show it off to people like a prize. Thinking I'm Spartacus when I'm just a fucking gangster. I don't want to get shot in the back of the head for something I probably never did, and spend ten years face-down in a bog in the middle of nowhere while my wife and child sit waiting, hoping, praying for me to come home. If that's the road to justice you can fucking bangle it.

SHANE. So it runs in the blood.

MICHAEL. Watch yourself there, Shane.

SHANE. I'm just saying. The apple don't fall that far.

MICHAEL. I said watch yourself.

DIARMAID. Now now, boys. We've all partaken.

SHANE *laughs*.

SHANE. You know what I think, young brothers. When you
    spend your week out here among the daisies and the
    butterflies, up on a haystack, picking your hole, watching the
    corn ripen... 'The swallows are eating the ladybirds.' 'I'll
    show you the right way to kill a goose.' Patsy O'Hara had
    fourteen fits the morning he died. Bit his tongue clean
    through. His soul on the edge of the void and he knew it,
    knew he was leaving this world, his family, his friends, and
    he closed his eyes shut and bit down. He did it for me, for
    Declan, for Diarmaid, for JJ and for you. This is not history.
    This is happening now. In two, three years when this war is
    really raging, and you're in town, walking down the old lane
    there and a car stops and Mr Muldoon gets out and asks you
    the question, what shall you tell him now? Or if I'm in
    McCartney's, and he asks me about you. What shall I say
    about you?

MICHAEL. I'm going to bed.

JJ. Me too.

DIARMAID. Ah, come on, boys. There's plenty of grog left.

SHANE. Nah, let 'em away. You sleep well now, Michael. You
    too, JJ. And make sure you get plenty of rest because there's
    lots and lots of work to do tomorrow. Them Polish pigs
    won't feed themselves.

MICHAEL *heads off. Stops*.

MICHAEL. If I'm walking down the old lane there and the car
    stops, I'll know what to say. And you better hope it's not a
    story I heard about a young boy getting hammered half to
    death in a house on the Palace Road. I don't know him as well
    as you, Shane, but I'm sure Mr Muldoon doesn't take kindly
    to stories like that doing the rounds. Did you ever think that

might have been the whole reason he brung you there? Just to
see how far the wind blows? Who knows, maybe all that boy
tied to the chair there did was watch a door once.

Pause.

What's the time there, Shane? Eh, son? What's the time?

Exit MICHAEL *and* JJ. *Silence.*

DECLAN. Well, you know what, fellas, I'm off to me
scratcher. There's work in the morning. And as the saying
goes, 'There's only so much whiskey a thirteen-year-old
boy can drink.'

He goes to leave.

Michael's right about one thing. Don't get me wrong, the
watch is fucking cool. But that thing round your neck? That
could be an unlucky omen there. That could bring bad luck
to a man. Goodnight, brothers.

He leaves.

DIARMAID *makes the noise of Windy Miller's windmill,
from* Camberwick Green. *He sings the first four lines of
his song.*

He laughs.

You fucking showed them there with the watch. I was
looking close and the keed's like, 'Aye, right hi…', then you
whip the watch out and I'm like, 'Have that up your hole.'
Did you see him? He was beaming. He's like…
(*Open-mouthed.*) Fucking cash till. Jaw on the floor.

SHANE. What are you doing asking me about Palace Road?

DIARMAID. What?

SHANE. That's classified. That's confidential, so it is.

DIARMAID. We was telling stories.

SHANE. You shouldn't have mentioned it.

DIARMAID. I didn't. You did.

SHANE. You fucking pestered me rotten.

DIARMAID. If it's so confidential why the fuck did you tell me in the first place?

SHANE. I've had a fuckin' drink, man.

DIARMAID. We'd all had a drink.

SHANE. He's here. Muldoon is here.

DIARMAID. Michael's not going to say nothing. He's stickin' it up you, so he is. Besides, there's no way on God's green earth Muldoon would come to them, ask them the question, like he come to us.

Pause.

SHANE. What?

DIARMAID. I mean he never would. Not in a million years.

SHANE. Mr Muldoon didn't come to *us*. He came to *me*.

DIARMAID. Of course he did. Sure, I never said different. What? I'm just saying.

SHANE. What are you saying?

DIARMAID. All I'm saying is there's no way Michael or JJ are ever stopped in the lane. So you can relax about the Palace Road. (*Beat.*) Although to be fair, if it had been me I wouldn't have told a fucking soul. I'm taking that shit to the sod, so I am.

SHANE *stares.*

I'm just saying. You spilled it up pretty quick. And 'pestered me rotten'... 'I'm sorry, Mr Muldoon, I was going to take that to my grave, except me little brother Diarmaid pestered me rotten.' Maybe Michael's got a point. Maybe it was a test. And let's face it, it didn't take long. I mean... It's not like I beat on you. It's not like I tied you to a fucking chair now.

SHANE *dives up and grabs his brother. They fight.*

Enter OISIN.

OISIN. Stop it. Stop it.

They see him.

DIARMAID. Will you leave off.

SHANE. Let go of me.

DIARMAID. Let go of me and I'll let go of you.

SHANE. Okay. One, two, three.

They break.

DIARMAID. Fuckin' eejit.

SHANE. Fuckin' prick.

Silence.

DIARMAID. All right, Oisin. You been for a walk?

SHANE. Nah, look at him. He's been listening. That's what you
do, isn't it, son? Listen at doors. In corners. You hear
everything now. Nothing gets past you.

DIARMAID. Leave the poor fucker alone.

SHANE. He's all right. You're all right, aren't you, Oisin?

OISIN *doesn't answer.*

DIARMAID. Your ma's out looking for you. She's up in the
wood there.

OISIN *doesn't answer.*

Well, I'm a little tired, a little drunk, and so, boys, I'm away
to my barn. And if you've any sense you'll do the same.

He sings some more of Windy Miller's song from
Camberwick Green. *He makes the sound of the windmill.
Burps. Exits.*

OISIN *and* SHANE *stand there. Silence.*

SHANE. You a whiskey man? Here.

He pours him some in a cup.

Drop of water? Lots of men do, and there's no shame to it.
It brings out the peat. Me, I like that punch in the back of the
throat. That fire. You want water?

OISIN. No.

SHANE. Good man. Here.

He gives him the whiskey.

Sláinte.

They drink.

OISIN. I wasn't listening at the door…

SHANE. Of course you weren't.

OISIN. I was next door. I could hear voices.

SHANE. We was all just talking shite anyway. Where've you been all evening?

OISIN. I went to the woods.

SHANE. Your ma's out looking for ya.

OISIN. Bollocks to my ma.

SHANE. Easy, big man.

OISIN. Fuck my ma. And fuck Uncle Quinn, too.

SHANE. Uncle Quinn. Sure, what's he done now?

OISIN. Uncle Quinn's a traitor. My da's dead because of him.

SHANE. Catch yourself on there, big man. Sure, Quinn took you in. And your ma. Every fuckin' spud you ever ate.

OISIN. He's a liar. A fuckin' liar.

SHANE. Sure, have another drink, big man. You've had bad news an' all. You'll need a few to get over something like that.

OISIN *takes the bottle. Drinks. Silence.*

OISIN. You went to Bobby's funeral.

SHANE. So you were listening. Sure enough, I was there. I saw the coffin. The shots over the grave.

OISIN. There's none here will talk about it. Only Aunt Pat. We sit up and she tells me the stories. I want to join the RA.

Pause. SHANE *laughs.*

SHANE. Well, hold your horses there, young fella.

OISIN. I'm serious.

SHANE. Because it's not that fucking easy. It's not the fucking Cubs.

OISIN. Everyone here pretends nothing is going on when I know exactly what's going on. A fuckin' blind man can see it. Do they think I'm fuckin' stupid? I've got eyes.

SHANE. Relax, man. Have a drink.

OISIN does.

Pause.

OISIN. Is that really Jimmy Muldoon's watch?

Silence.

SHANE. Can I ask you a question. The Englishman over there. The one in the cottage.

OISIN. Tom Kettle.

SHANE. What's the situation between him and your ma?

OISIN. What do you mean?

SHANE. Search me. Seems like he's sweet on her or something.

OISIN. I don't know.

SHANE. You sure about that?

Pause.

OISIN. Tom Kettle looks at my ma's legs.

Pause.

SHANE. See, that's one thing I've never understood. Why Quinn keeps an Englishmen there. Over there in the cottage.

OISIN. Search me.

SHANE. Is it to ogle your ma's breasts? Look up her skirt?

OISIN. I don't fuckin' know.

SHANE. Well, I'll tell you what I know. I came through here late this evening, and you know what I saw. Tom Kettle down on one knee in front of your ma. The filthy cunt can't wait for the sun to go down once before he's jumping in your dad's bed…

Pause.

OISIN. He's a snake.

Beat.

SHANE. An Englishman. On one knee to your mam. The same day she finds she's a widow. The same fucking day.

OISIN. On his knee?

Beat.

SHANE. Do you know if he locks his door at night?

Pause.

OISIN. Why?

SHANE. Don't tell me you haven't snuck in there once or twice.

OISIN. He doesn't lock it. It's always open.

SHANE. Where does Quinn keep that shotgun?

Pause.

Is it still in the cabinet there in the back?

OISIN. It's locked.

SHANE. Right.

OISIN. Sure, we've tried to find the key for years to take it out and shoot an old badger, or fox or something.

SHANE. Well, that's that then. If there's no key. But if we knew where Uncle Quinn kept the key, then a man might do something tonight. A man who wanted justice.

Pause.

OISIN. Aunt Pat keeps a pistol.

Pause.

SHANE. Where?

OISIN. Under her bed. In an old suitcase. It belonged to her brother.

SHANE. Have you looked inside?

OISIN. Lots of times.

SHANE. Does it have bullets?

OISIN. Three. I can unload it and reload it.

Silence.

SHANE. Well, that's that. I'm away to my bed. There's a stack of jobs need fettling, and I'm gonna be stiff as a fucking board come sun-up. With a fucking pounder and no mistake.

He ruffles OISIN's *hair.*

Mr Muldoon respects action. Not talk. Because the truth, Oisin. The truth travels. If you're listening you can hear it loud and clear. 'I am hungry only for justice.'

SHANE *picks up the whiskey bottle.*

Sleep well, boy. Sleep well now.

He leaves to the outside.

AUNT MAGGIE *enters. She is in some distress. She mutters to herself, pointing at the window.*

AUNT MAGGIE. There's something… There's something there… What's out there?

She moves closer to the window.

OISIN *exits into the parlour.*

Is there something out there?

Enter HORRIGAN. *He hasn't slept.*

AUNT MAGGIE *turns to face him.*

Daddy, is that you?

HORRIGAN. It's Father Horrigan, Maggie.

Pause.

AUNT MAGGIE. Who's that?

HORRIGAN. It's Father Horrigan…

Pause.

AUNT MAGGIE. I'm scared, Daddy.

HORRIGAN. Why are you scared, Maggie?

Pause.

AUNT MAGGIE. There's something… Can you not hear that
sound?

HORRIGAN. What sound is that?

AUNT MAGGIE. Far off. But it's coming closer. I know that
sound. I heard it long ago. They're coming.

Pause.

HORRIGAN. Let's put you through here now, Aunt Maggie. I'll
light the stove there and we'll wrap you in a nice blanket.

AUNT MAGGIE *begins to sing 'Eilean Mo Chridh' ('Isle of
My Heart').*

HORRIGAN *helps her through to the parlour. The kitchen is
empty.*

From next door, AUNT MAGGIE *singing. 'Eilean Mo
Chridh'.*

Enter UNCLE PAT.

He pours himself a glass of water. He tops it up with whiskey.

He stands for a beat, listening to the singing.

Enter HORRIGAN.

UNCLE PAT. Father.

HORRIGAN. Patrick. Good evening. I was just lighting the
stove for Maggie there.

UNCLE PAT. Is she warm?

HORRIGAN. Aye, she's warm.

UNCLE PAT. Sure, it's awfully late, Father.

Beat.

HORRIGAN. I just heard the news about Seamus. I felt I should come. In case there were any in the household who needed their priest.

UNCLE PAT. Of course. Of course. I'm afraid they're all asleep.

HORRIGAN. I'll wait in here. I'll not disturb anyone.

UNCLE PAT. Will you not have a drop?

HORRIGAN. Thank you. No.

The singing stops.

UNCLE PAT. I love hearing her sing like that. She always used to sing. Big Jack used to call her his little nightingale.

Pause.

It's been a strange day, so it has. Such terrible news. After all this time.

HORRIGAN. Terrible.

UNCLE PAT. I was putting young Mercy to bed earlier and she said to me, 'Uncle Pat, where has Seamus been all this time? Where has his soul been?' And I opened my mouth to answer. But nothing came. I had no answer. In case she asks again, I was wondering what to say. Where would you say his soul has been, Father. Where has it been?

Silence.

HORRIGAN. Seamus's soul will soon be at rest.

UNCLE PAT *nods. Pause.*

UNCLE PAT. Are you familiar with Virgil, Father? (*Holds up his book.*) More and more I find myself, up in the wee hours, sharing a drop of Bushmills with the Ancients. *The Aeneid.* In which our hero ventures to the Underworld, and crossing over the River Styx, spies a crowd of people on the far bank?

HORRIGAN. I'm not sure I recall it, no.

Pause.

UNCLE PAT (*reads*). 'Here all the crowd streams, hurrying to the shores, women and men, pleading to make the crossing, stretching out their hands in longing for the far shore.

But the boatman rows on. Aeneas, stirred and astonished at the tumult, said. "O virgin, tell me, what does this crowding to the river mean?

What do the souls want?" The ancient priestess replied…

As UNCLE PAT *closes the book and intones from memory, enter* QUINN, *from upstairs, unseen. He is dressed differently.*

"Son of Anchises, true child of the gods, all this crowd, you see, they are the unburied. The ferryman is Charon. He may not carry them from the fearful shore on the harsh waters before their bones are at rest in the earth. They roam for a thousand years lost on these shores, their souls abandoned. Only then are they admitted, and revisit the pools they long for."'

Silence.

QUINN. Who's there?

UNCLE PAT. Fear not, Quinn. It's that old fool Pat, and the Father…

HORRIGAN. I left my car down by the bottom gate. I walked up. I didn't want to –

UNCLE PAT. The Father just heard the news about poor Seamus. He didn't want to wait.

QUINN. Is that right, Pat? Sure, it was the Father who told me about Seamus. When he came this morning.

Pause.

UNCLE PAT. Well, I'll be off to bed. If Maggie stirs, I'll not be sleeping.

QUINN. Goodnight, Pat.

HORRIGAN. Goodnight, Pat.

UNCLE PAT *goes to leave.*

UNCLE PAT. Our friend Virgil has it that there's only two types of souls forbidden passage to the beyond. The unburied. And liars. Those that lie to the innocent. Goodnight, Father.

He exits upstairs.

QUINN. What do you want?

HORRIGAN. May I please sit?

QUINN. No you may fucking not sit. I told you to leave this family alone. If you're here in the middle of the night, you're here for one reason. Now say what he told you to say and leave.

HORRIGAN. Quinn –

QUINN. Do it, priest. Run your errand.

Pause.

HORRIGAN. He came to my house tonight. He wants your assurance that Seamus's death… That your brother's death –

QUINN (*interrupting*). He has my answer. The answer is no.

Pause.

HORRIGAN. Then it's not you I need to speak to, Quinn. (*Beat.*) It's Mary.

Beat.

QUINN. And what would you have to say to Mary? (*Beat.*) What would you have to say to Mary, Father?

HORRIGAN. It's about Caitlin.

Beat.

QUINN. What about Caitlin?

HORRIGAN. She told me.

Silence.

Quinn. Caitlin is in love with you. She's been in love with you for years.

Pause.

QUINN. Sure, Mickey Horrigan, you're a fuckin' snake, so you are. Why do you come here with this mischief? These fucking lies, man. Have you no shame left?

HORRIGAN. She's been telling me for years.

QUINN. Ah... you fucking idiot. You fucking... Was this her confession? Have you just broken the Sacrament of Penance? Ah, Mickey... I know you're a weak man... But tell me you haven't just sent your fucking soul to Hell. Tell me it's a lie. Just say it.

HORRIGAN. He showed me a photograph... My sister. She's all I have. (*Beat.*) You're a good man, Quinn Carney. A good man.

Enter MARY *from upstairs.*

MARY. Quinn? Is everything all right?

QUINN (*low, to* HORRIGAN). Make your choice, Mickey. Make your choice.

MARY. Is that you, Father? It's not yet six. Sure, what brings you here at such an hour? What's wrong?

Pause.

HORRIGAN. It's all right, Mary. Nothing's wrong.

MARY. Then why are you here? What's going on?

HORRIGAN. Sure, Quinn telephoned me. He needed to speak to me. About Seamus. He needed his priest.

Beat.

MARY. Of course. Well, that's good now. It was good of you to come. You've been a rock for this family for longer than I can remember.

HORRIGAN. Thank you, Mary.

QUINN. Father Horrigan was just leaving.

MARY. Surely we can have a quick cuppa?

HORRIGAN. Thank you, Mary. But I must prepare for mass. Good morning, Mary. Good morning, Quinn. God be with you.

QUINN. And with you, Father. And with you.

MARY. I'll show you out.

> HORRIGAN *leaves with* MARY.
>
> QUINN *is alone.*
>
> MARY *re-enters.*
>
> Are the boys all in bed?

QUINN. They're away in the barn there.

MARY. Good.

> *Pause.*
>
> I'm glad you did that, Quinn.

QUINN. Did what?

MARY. Called Father Horrigan. If I've a worry about you,
Quinn, it's that you keep it all in. You hold it inside.
Telephoning the Father, sharing the burden. I'm proud of you.

> *Pause.*
>
> How is Caitlin?

QUINN. We've hardly spoken.

MARY. Well, I'm sure it must all be sinking in.

> *Pause.*
>
> I know you talk to Caitlin. Discuss things. Has she ever
> made clear what her plans are?

QUINN. Plans?

MARY. I mean after the funeral. After the dust settles, I think the
first thing that should happen, is Caitlin should find a place of
her own. Sure, she needs a fresh start. I have some savings.
My share of the money Big Jack left us. I have it in the post
office. I'm going to use a portion of it to give to Caitlin, so
she can get herself up on her feet. It'll go some way, if she
doesn't fritter it. Spend half of it on whiskey. I intend to
mention that when I give her the money. That's my one
stipulation. Apart from anything else, what sort of example

does carrying on like that set the wean? Oisin's problems do
not begin and end with Seamus's vanishing.

Pause.

QUINN. That's a powerful word. Vanishing.

Pause.

Have you not vanished, Mary?

Pause.

MARY. How do you mean?

QUINN. Up there, in your room, the radio on, day after day.
Not dressing.

MARY. Sure, I've not been well. With the viruses.

QUINN. You don't have a virus, Mary. There are no viruses.

MARY. Are you saying I choose to be this way? I choose to be
up there?

QUINN. Do you not? Sure, it's years since you were part of this
family.

MARY. I don't want to talk about this. This is not the
conversation we should be having.

QUINN *laughs.*

QUINN. 'This is not the conversation we should be having.'
(*Beat.*) Six, seven years ago. The bed and breakfast in Cork.
In the morning on the quay I asked you what was wrong.
I wanted to talk about how things were. Between us. You
said, 'This is not the conversation we should be having.'
(*Beat.*) A year later I stopped the car. I said we needed to
talk. When I look at you, you look away. You won't look me
in the eye. You said, 'This is not the conversation we should
be having.' (*Beat.*) Last harvest. That morning, with the
rainbow. Out the window of the bedroom up there. And we
went outside with our cups of tea and with every one of our
children still asleep, we looked at the rainbow and I tried to
speak. About how if we weren't close and all, at least we
could be a family. If you'd come down and share it. Just be
a part of it. You said, 'This is not the conversation we

should be having.' Which begs the question, Mary, *what exactly is the conversation we should be fucking having*?

Pause.

MARY. We said two or three months. But she was so desperate, so lost, so shaken by the not knowing, by the grief that couldn't be grief, that after six months the situation was worse. Nothing was healing. Nothing was moving on. We both said that this was kindness. The Christian thing to do. Oisin had brothers. Sisters. She was your brother's wife. Or widow. We didn't know. She didn't know. And as time went on and the months became years, years of not knowing, less wife, more widow? Or perhaps… Perhaps… just a woman. A young, beautiful woman. Under this roof. Who made you smile. Who knew how to make you laugh. I didn't know the words to say to make you smile. I did once, but somewhere, among all those weeks and months of waiting and nothing healing and the same days and the same waiting, somewhere there I forgot how to make you smile. I forgot how to make you laugh. Now it's over. Now there's a body. Now she can grieve. Now she can mourn. Now, Quinn. Now we can move on. Now look me in the eye and say that is something you want.

Pause.

If I were to stand here, Quinn, and speak my heart. If I were to show you who I am, is that something you'd even want?

Pause.

Why was the Father really here?

Pause.

QUINN. I can't say.

MARY *stands, she holds her husband's face.*

MARY. What's the matter, Quinn? Have you vanished?

Silence.

Enter CAITLIN *from outside.*

Good morning, Cait. You're up early.

CAITLIN. I'm looking for Oisin. Have you seen him?

MARY. I haven't seen him. Have you seen him, Quinn?

QUINN. No.

MARY. Is he not in the barn with the Corcorans?

CAITLIN. No he's not.

MARY. I'm sure he'll turn up. He usually does. Well, I'm off back to bed.

CAITLIN. Goodnight, Mary.

MARY. Sure, it's nearly the morning, Cait. By the way. I'm feeling a little better. So I'll be making the Harvest Breakfast myself this morning.

CAITLIN. Very good, Mary. And I'm glad to hear you're feeling better.

MARY. You know what, I am. I am feeling better. I think this virus may finally be lifting.

Exit MARY.

Beat.

QUINN. Did you find him?

CAITLIN. Father Horrigan's car is parked at the gate.

Pause.

QUINN. Aye, he came.

CAITLIN. What did he want?

QUINN. He wanted to talk about the funeral.

CAITLIN. What did he really want?

Pause.

Why did he come here, Quinn? What did he say to you?

Pause.

He told you. Didn't he?

Pause. He nods.

Did he leave anything out?

QUINN *shakes his head once.*

Beat.

Well, let's look on the bright side. At least Father Horrigan is going to Hell.

Silence.

Well, that's that then.

QUINN. I feel exactly the same.

Pause.

CAITLIN. Well, that makes it all all right then. All we have to do is run away together.

Pause.

QUINN. I've been carrying it. Day and night for years. I told myself it was bollocks… To wise up. And I did. I did wise up. I shut it out. So why did every smile, every smile of my every child, every bedtime song. Every picture on this wall. Their shoes. I look at their shoes and I want to fuckin' die. I look at their coats. Their mittens. Their fucking… I take the girls swimming. And they wave from the water and I wave back. I swear I'd take a fuckin' kneecapping over that.

Pause.

And Mary. Every time it rains. Every time the sun comes out. Every time anything fucking ever fuckin' happens, fuckin' any time, ever.

CAITLIN. I have no fuckin' idea what you're talking about.

QUINN. Me either. It's all bollocks. It's all bollocks.

Pause.

Then I look at you.

CAITLIN. Sure, I wish to God right now we'd been riding each other ragged for years.

QUINN. I couldn't agree more.

Pause.

Muldoon knows. It was him sent the Father…

CAITLIN. What does he want?

QUINN. A lie. That Seamus just vanished.

Pause.

CAITLIN. Well, if that's what he wants then that's what we'll give him.

QUINN. No –

CAITLIN. Quinn –

QUINN. I can't do it. Not after all you've been through.

CAITLIN. What difference does it make?

QUINN. It's a *lie*, Cait. A fucking lie –

CAITLIN. If that's what it takes –

QUINN. No –

CAITLIN. If that's the price. If that's what it takes to leave this family be.

QUINN. It was me made Seamus join up. We sat in here. Night after night… In this room. Me talking, him sat there, with the whiskey and the wide eyes. Soaking it up. I was so fuckin' sure.

CAITLIN. No –

QUINN. I walked away for this family. What have I done? I built this. All of it. I built it all.

She holds his hands. Intently.

CAITLIN. Now you listen to me. (*Beat.*) If there is another world, a secret world, where everything is right and proper and perfect and as it should be… Then in that world I am not with Seamus Carney. You built the only happiness I have ever known. And I know it's not real. I know it's not. But it's *there*. It's fuckin' there. I can see it.

She holds his face.

Know this, Quinn Carney. I love you more than the future. Because in the future we cannot be. So kiss me, and then it is the future. Where we are not. Where we can never be.

They kiss.

When I'm old… when I've forgotten my own face, the shape of my hands, or what those hands did. I will remember your face. Your hands. And that's enough for me. That's enough. Go to your family now. Save your family.

MAGENNIS. Good morning.

MAGENNIS is standing there. In the shadows. QUINN stands. Enter MALONE and MULDOON.

MULDOON. Good morning, Quinn. Caitlin. You're up early.

MAGENNIS. It's not early. It's late.

MULDOON. Please forgive me. I have to be back in town later this morning so you'll excuse me if I press forward. Have you considered my request?

Beat. MARY appears on the stairs. QUINN stands looking only at CAITLIN.

QUINN. I have.

MULDOON. And –

Pause.

QUINN *looks at* CAITLIN.

QUINN. I accept that neither you, nor anyone you know, was involved in the disappearance of Seamus Carney. (*Beat.*) That no one from this family will speak on the subject. No one will talk to the press. No one will breathe a word to anyone. It's in the past and it will stay in the past. I give you this assurance, in return for one of my own.

He turns to face MULDOON.

That when you leave this house, you will allow us to bury Seamus in peace. To grieve in peace. If you can give me this assurance then you have my word. (*Beat.*) You have my word.

Pause.

MULDOON. Well, I have to say thank you, Quinn. It means a great deal that you would see sense at this difficult time.

The sacrifice this family made, the suffering it has undergone, is real. It will not be forgotten. And to show that thanks, I've decided to help you. To help this family. With Caitlin.

QUINN. What do you mean?

MULDOON. There's the maisonette there in the Bishops Road in Derry. It has two bedrooms downstairs. And a living room and a kitchenette with a hatch. It's got a brand-new set of PVC windows. I want Caitlin and her boy to move in there. It's our way of showing that, whereas we bear no responsibility for what happened, there are also no hard feelings. Caitlin's rent would be provided for the first year, and she would be under my personal protection. It would mean that you and Mary can have the space that a man and his wife should have, space for you and her and your family.

QUINN. This family can take care of its own.

MULDOON. We think it's important to demonstrate to the wider community that we take care of our own. We regard Seamus as one of our own. So I'm afraid it's not up for negotiation.

QUINN. The answer is no.

MARY. Quinn –

MULDOON. I don't think you understand, Quinn. This isn't a debate. I'm not canvassing your opinion, or seeking your wise guidance. I'm informing you. I will be taking care of Caitlin Carney. And you will capitulate. You will do exactly what I require of you, or you will give me no option but to reverse my policy of goodwill towards this family. I suggest you do it. For Honor. Mercy. Shena. Nuala. James Joseph. Michael. Bobby. (*Beat.*) Mary.

CAITLIN. Thank you, Mr Muldoon. I accept your offer.

Beat. They all turn. CAITLIN *is standing there. She is shaking.*

QUINN. Cait.

CAITLIN. Mr Muldoon is right. This is the chance for me and Oisin to put this all behind us. To move on.

QUINN. No.

CAITLIN. It's my decision. My choice. I accept your offer. And I thank you for the kindness you've shown me and my son.

MULDOON. Thank you, Caitlin.

MARY. Well, now. That's settled.

Enter SHANE, *from outside. He sings the first couple of lines of 'Teenage Kicks' by The Undertones.*

He has the whiskey bottle. It's empty. He sways under its effect, focusing.

SHANE. What's this, Uncle Quinn...? Are we having a wee party?

MARY. Go to bed, Shane.

SHANE. Aunt Cait. Now then. Now. Let's put a song on now. Aunt Cait. Would you like to dance now... I'm a fine dancer. And so are you.

MARY. You go to bed now, Shane.

SHANE *focuses blearily.*

SHANE. Mr Muldoon. Are you still here now? Will you have a drink with me?

MULDOON. That's enough, Shane.

SHANE. Jeez, do you remember those helicopters, Mr Muldoon? There at the funeral. Sure, they were deafening, so they were...

MAGENNIS. Mr Muldoon...?

MULDOON. It's all right, Frank.

SHANE. Well, I'm glad you're here because I have a question. That boy. The one in the Palace Road. Your man tied to the chair now.

MARY. Shane –

SHANE. I've been thinking about him. That boy. And I need to know. Where is he now? Where is that boy?

MALONE. You're drunk.

MAGENNIS. Say the word, Mr Muldoon.

SHANE. Where is he, Mr Muldoon? Is he okay? Is he
somewhere safe? Has he come good? I need to know.

MULDOON. I think you should sleep this off. Have a good
think in the morn–

SHANE. I've been thinking, see, and I don't think I want this.
I don't want it.

He pulls the chain from his neck. He holds it out.

MULDOON. What's that?

SHANE. What is that? What is that?

He throws it at MULDOON'*s feet.*

CAITLIN. Shane –

MARY. Shane –

MULDOON. Relax, Frank.

MALONE. Easy, paperboy.

SHANE stands in front of MALONE.

SHANE. What did you say? Paperboy? Fucking… paperboy?
I'm a fucking warrior. I can do this. I'm fucking ready.
(*To* MULDOON.) What's the plan, big man? Where do you
want me, skipper? I'll do anything! I'm a fucking lion!
I flinch at nothing! I'm ready! Give me the order! GIVE ME
THE ORDER!

A terrible howling from outside.

Enter TOM KETTLE, *holding* OISIN'*s body.*

CAITLIN. Oisin!

TOM KETTLE. I was sleeping.

CAITLIN. What happened?

MARY. Oisin?

CAITLIN. Oisin?

MARY. What happened, Tom?

TOM KETTLE. He said he wanted to kill me.

CAITLIN. Wake up, Oisin! Oisin! Wake up!

Enter JJ *from upstairs.*

JJ. What's happened? What's going on?

TOM KETTLE. He was shouting and screaming. He had this.

TOM KETTLE *holds up the gun.*

CAITLIN. Wake up, Oisin! Up you get.

TOM KETTLE. He was shouting, 'Mr Muldoon is here.' It was very loud. I thought, I better do something. So I wrung his neck.

CAITLIN. No, no, no! Oisin! Oh my God!

TOM KETTLE. Just last week we put the window back.

MICHAEL *and the* GIRLS *appear at the top of the stairs.*

MICHAEL. Aunt Cait, what's happened?

TOM KETTLE. All morning, just us.

CAITLIN. It's all right, Oisin. It's all right.

MULDOON. Caitlin.

Enter AUNT PAT.

AUNT PAT. What's happening?

DIARMAID *and* DECLAN *appear.*

DIARMAID. What's happened, Aunt Cait?

CAITLIN. It's all right. It's all right.

MICHAEL. Jesus, he's not breathing, Auntie Cait.

CAITLIN *picks up the razor from the shelf with the stereo on it. Behind her back.*

CAITLIN. It's all right.

MICHAEL. He's not breathing.

CAITLIN. It's all right. It's all right.

CAITLIN rushes at MULDOON. QUINN stops her, at the last moment.

QUINN. No. Caitlin. No.

CAITLIN. You bastard!

QUINN. No. No. Sssshh. It's all right. It's all right.

He takes the razor from her. QUINN turns.

MULDOON. Quinn, that is not what I'd hoped f–

MARY. No!

QUINN slashes MULDOON's throat. Blood spurts two feet. MULDOON begins very quickly to bleed to death.

QUINN turns, grabs the pistol and fires it at MAGENNIS, hitting him in the forehead. His blood spurts all over the wall of family pictures.

DIARMAID. Holy Jesus.

MULDOON drops to his knees.

MULDOON (*looking at* QUINN). There now. (*Beat.*) There he is. (*Beat.*) Quinn Carney.

AUNT PAT. What have you done?

UNCLE PAT. Quinn?

QUINN aims at MALONE.

QUINN. Go back to town. Tell whoever you need to tell, that this day, Quinn Carney has exacted revenge for the murder of Seamus Carney. Husband to Caitlin. Father to Oisin. Tell whoever comes here to come ready. Now go.

Exit MALONE.

AUNT MAGGIE appears in the parlour doorway. She is standing, alert.

In the distance, a sound. The lights flicker again.

MULDOON *dies.*

AUNT MAGGIE. They're coming.

CAITLIN. Sssh, now, my love. Rest now, my love. Ssshhh…

AUNT PAT. What have you done, Quinn? What have you done to this family?

AUNT MAGGIE. They're coming.

CAITLIN *kneels over* OISIN*'s body.*

The sound getting closer. Screaming.

JJ. Dad. What will we do? What will we do…?

MICHAEL. What will we do, Dad?

The screaming builds.

AUNT MAGGIE. They're here…!

Outside, the Banshees scream. It rises.

They're here…!

The screams rise.

They're here!

The screams rise.

The final candle flickers and dies. And as it does –

Silence.

Darkness.

Curtain.

The End.

JEZ BUTTERWORTH

Mojo (1995), *The Night Heron* (2002), *The Winterling* (2006), *Jerusalem* (2009), *The River* (2012) and *The Ferryman* (2017) were all premiered at the Royal Court Theatre, London. *The Ferryman* transferred to the Gielgud Theatre in London's West End later in 2017. *Jerusalem* transferred to the Apollo Theatre, West End in 2010, the Music Box Theatre, New York, in 2011, and back to the Apollo later in 2011. *Parlour Song* was premiered at the Atlantic Theater, New York, in 2008, and at the Almeida Theatre, London, in 2009. *Mojo* won the George Devine Award, the Olivier Award for Best Comedy and the Writers' Guild, Critics' Circle and Evening Standard Awards for Most Promising Playwright. It was revived at the Harold Pinter Theatre in the West End in 2013. *Jerusalem* won the Best Play Award at the Critics' Circle, Evening Standard and WhatsOnStage.com Awards, and was nominated for the Tony Award for Best Play. Jez wrote and directed the film adaptation of *Mojo* (1998), starring Ian Hart and Harold Pinter, and *Birthday Girl* (2002), starring Nicole Kidman and Ben Chaplin, and co-wrote and produced *Fair Game* (2010), starring Sean Penn and Naomi Watts. In 2007 he was awarded the E. M. Forster Award by the American Academy of Arts and Letters.